Perfectly Hugo

Praise for Perfectly Hugo

"Equal parts heartwarming and bittersweet, Monier's novel reimagines the universal experience of grief through the lens of technology, addressing both the comfort and the uncanniness that AI can bring. A touching meditation on love and loss in a futuristic world that may be closer than one thinks."

—Kirkus Reviews

"Author Barbara Monier has crafted an absorbing narrative about the moral, philosophical, and emotional implications of advanced AI technology on everyday human lives. It's a character-driven story about a couple deeply in love, trying to deal with the inevitable nature of loss and human mortality. Monier's character work is stellar. I…highly recommend it."

—Reviewed by Pikasho Deka for Readers' Favorite

"Barbara Monier's latest novel, *Perfectly Hugo,* is the most thought-provoking novel I have read in a long time."

—Len Joy, author of The Stonemason Trilogy

Perfectly Hugo is the kind of novel that dares the reader to consider what our world might become if we forget or dismiss the very things that keep us human."

—David W. Berner, The Writer's Shed Reviews

"The book is a meditation on grief, filled with an eye for nature, an ear for the habits and patterns of conversation that bind two people…"

—James R. Petersen, Moth Story Slam Champion

"Pitch-perfect blend of literary wit, believable dialogue, and psychological insight."

—Brooke Laufer, *The Age of the Too Good Mother (2026)*

"The ending…is perfect. I'm in awe."

—Carol Orange, *A Discerning Eye*

"This one will rock you hard and stay with you."

—Rita Dragonette, *The Fourteenth of September*

"Brilliant…what exactly makes up the thing called human intimacy? Monier's story explores these questions and much more."

—Ruth Hull Chatlien, *Katie, Bar the Door*

"A prescient novel…a powerful meditation on the experience of aging, when the hope for new beginnings is weighed against the pull of the past."

—Molly Hales, *Vital Ties* (2026)

"A superb, quietly magical story that should not be missed by anyone who has ever loved."

—Pat Camalliere, author of The Cora Tozzi Historical Mystery Series

"A book for our time! Packed with movement and depth."

—Patricia Shevlin, *My NUNcommon Life*

"Exquisitely crafted and beautifully executed. It is short, but long enough to provide humor and insight without extraneous elements or diversions."

—M.H.

"Exceptionally rich, nuanced and inventive."

—Jan Seriff Berger

"Beautiful imagery is the star of Barbara Monier's new novel."

—R.D.

"A perfectly satisfying read."

—Debbie Pavick

Also by Barbara Monier

The Reading

The Rocky Orchard

Pushing the River

A Little Birdie Told Me

You, in Your Green Shirt

Perfectly Hugo

A novel

Barbara Monier

Paperback First Edition ISBN 978-1-956872-87-3

Ebook First Edition ISBN 978-1-956872-58-3

AMIKA PRESS 2444 Pioneer Road, Evanston, IL 60201 847 920 8084

info@amikapress.com Available for purchase on amikapress.com

Cover illustration © Copyright 2025, Barbara Monier, generated by Canva AI. Cover design by Beth O'Driscoll. Author photography by Mac. Designed & typeset by Beth O'Driscoll.

The worst part of holding the memories is not the pain.
It's the loneliness of it.
Memories need to be shared.

—*Lois Lowry*

But tell me you love me, come back and haunt me
Oh, and I rush to the start
Runnin' in circles, chasin' our tails
Coming back as we are

—*Chris Martin, Guy Berryman, William Champion, Jonathan Buckland*

1

Enid would go over the two hours of that late October afternoon a thousand times. A thousand times she would sit in that same chair by that same window, recounting the events, replaying minute details of one hundred twenty minutes over and over in her head. A thousand times she would ask herself: what was her first inkling? What was the first thing that had stirred her, had awakened some part of her that sensed the future?

A string of events was about to unfold. Her life would not be the same. And she would have one year, three hundred sixty-five days, to make a decision.

2

Enid adjusted the sun visor for the third time in ten minutes, trying in vain to block the late-afternoon glare. She exhaled sharply, more out of habit than necessity, and flicked the turn signal. The little green arrow on the dashboard ticked rhythmically.

Hugo smiled.

Without turning her head, Enid said, "What's so damn funny?"

"I'm not laughing."

"You're smiling. At my expense, I'm thinking," Enid said.

"You're fidgeting," Hugo said, his voice easy, warm.

"No I'm not." Enid thought for a second. "I am?"

"Oh, yeah." Hugo looked her up and down. "You're not even sitting the way you usually do. Plus you have *both hands* on the wheel."

"You've been yelling at me for years to do that!"

"Not yelling." Hugo sighed and ran his hand through his hair, "I don't yell at you, Enid."

"You're right," she said, "Sorry."

Neither one of them said anything for a time. Enid removed one of her hands from the steering wheel. She placed the hand on her thigh, then moved it to rest on the center console. She cleared her throat and put her hand back on the steering wheel. "Forget it," she said. "Today you get your lifelong wish. Both hands on the wheel."

Hugo laughed. "I thought if you drove it might help. Thought maybe you'd be *less* fidgety," Hugo said.

Enid pressed her lips together. "I'm not fidgety, exactly. I'm just—"

"Nervous," Hugo supplied, tilting his head toward her. He stretched out his legs, settling more comfortably into the passenger seat. His hands rested on his stomach, but his fingers tapped rat-a-tat against his jacket.

"I just… I don't have any idea what to expect from these… people. What if they're—"

"Assembled?" Hugo grinned.

"Very funny," Enid said.

"It was right there. Low-hanging fruit."

"And stop interrupting me," Enid said. "That was the second time."

"Sorry," Hugo said quickly. "About interrupting. Really."

She huffed, but not the kind that meant irritation. She glanced at him briefly before refocusing on the road. "So, I'm fidgety, and you're sort of… weirdly determined to act relaxed. I mean, come on, this couldn't be a much more bizarre situation."

"Agreed."

"What if… what if we don't like this whole thing? What if they don't like us!"

"We're pretty likeable."

"Hugo, I'm serious. I'm a little… freaked out here. OK, more than a little."

"About what?"

"About *what?* Are you kidding?"

"I meant specifically. Is there specific stuff you're freaked out about? 'Cause, Enid, for God's sake. we've been over and over and over all this." Hugo circled his head around as he spoke. "The decision to do this. To come here."

"Now you're mad at me," Enid said.

"Not that much." Hugo examined his fingernails. "Mildly annoyed, is all. Waiting to hear what's 'freaking you out.'"

"I don't know." Enid looked over at him then glanced out the passenger side window beyond him. "I hate this part. This endless stretch of dreary city. Ivy calls it 'eternal winter.'"

Hugo drummed his fingers in the center of the dashboard. "Still waiting," he said.

"Maybe they have rules, or some sort of… expectations we don't meet. What if we get in there and realize the whole shebang is completely ridiculous?"

"Then we leave," Hugo's voice was gentle. "We get back in this very car, go home, and watch something really stupid on television. Maybe we make some toast."

"Toast? That's your fallback plan?"

"Toast can be the perfect thing for people who are… retreating from something. Or need comfort. It's easy. It's soothing. You can eat it in silence, reflecting on your mistakes. Or you can just go pleasantly blank."

Enid couldn't help but laugh. "Never know which Hugo is gonna come out of your mouth. Philosopher poet? Comedian wannabe?

"Never sure myself. Right now, I'm a man in a car with his wife, headed toward something new. We're good at that, Enid. Always have been."

She absorbed that for a moment. He was right. They had built a life on small and large leaps alike—buying their first house, changing careers, befriending people they never expected to, finding joy in places they'd once dismissed. Maybe this was just another one of those leaps.

The traffic light ahead turned red. Enid eased the car to a stop, glancing at the GPS on the dashboard. "Two more blocks."

"Exciting."

"Or regrettable."

"Still exciting."

She tapped her fingers against the steering wheel. "Are you really not even a little jittery? Nervous? Something like that?"

Hugo considered. "I suppose I am. A little. I figure, either it's a world of weirdness and we make an interesting memory, or it's something that feels right, and we find a place, a possibility. Maybe somewhere we belong. No downside."

"You're very… glass-half-full about this."

"Isn't my glass usually about three-quarters full? I'm pretty sure you count on that."

"Fair," Enid said. "But the toast thing? You really don't have to try quite so hard. To shore me up."

"Fair," Hugo said.

The light turned green. Enid took a breath, released it, and pressed the gas pedal.

Two blocks later, Enid pulled the car into a small parking lot, the back of which was lined with a perfect row of stately old white pines. To the side lay a winding path with a garden border that looked like it had been plucked whole from an English cottage. Enid put the car in park but didn't turn off the engine. She stared through the windshield. "This is it," she said. The building at the end of the path exhibited a humble charm that matched the garden. It looked to have once been a rambling old house, perhaps from the late 1800s. A modest sign near the door read "Assembled Souls—Welcome." The words were painted in a cheerful teal. The lettering was faded, meant to appear slightly worn by time. Enid knew Assembled Souls—the entire enterprise—was less than two years old.

Hugo nodded, looking it over. "Way less tech-y than I expected. Less cult-y, too."

"Cult-y?"

"What? It's a fair observation."

Enid sighed, then checked the rearview mirror unnecessarily, delaying the inevitable. "All right. Let's do this."

She turned off the car. Hugo reached over and squeezed her hand. "No toast tonight."

"No toast tonight," she agreed. She lingered in the feeling of his hand's warmth, the weight of it on her own.

Hugo got out of the car and began walking toward the door. Enid closed the door behind her and clapped her hands together. "Bring on the Merchants of Death!" she said.

"Merchants of Death! Jesus Christ, Enid!"

Enid thought she heard a genuine flash of anger in Hugo's voice, but when he took a couple of steps toward her, he saw the tears that had formed. He walked over and stood directly in front of her. He placed a hand on each of her cheeks and looked into her eyes. "We're together, Enid," Hugo said. "We're doing this together."

"We're together now. But we're doing this for… for…"

"I'm right here."

"For now," she said. "You are for now."

"Come on." Hugo took Enid's hand in his and began walking toward the building. "Let's give this a go."

"I didn't expect the speculative future to look so cottage-core," Enid whispered.

Hugo chuckled. "Maybe they redesign the look of the place for every new person or couple who comes in."

"The outside, too? It's all pretty consistent. So far." Enid said.

"Who knows? Maybe this is all an elaborate illusion. Wouldn't it be weird if everything had been whipped up by a 3-D printer moments before we arrived?"

"You're starting to get annoying in your attempts to be comforting." Enid's voice had no annoyance in it, and she inwardly acknowledged that she did find comfort in Hugo's comedic ease. She always had. "But seriously, I did wonder if this building's actually old. Did you notice the sign? The washed-out lettering? This company's only two years old."

"Yep."

Once inside, Enid and Hugo waited at the entrance to the room, taking in the dark oak woodwork, the mantle and fireplace, the packed bookshelves. "If they do change it for each visitor, the English cottage design is a nod to you, my dear."

"You're kidding, right? You love the homey, cozy, firelit, bookshelf-lined, wood-centric look!" Enid said. "I mean, this looks freakishly like our *house*." She shot Hugo a suspicious look. "Are you saying they would have chosen a different décor for you? If it were just you here?"

"Yes," Hugo responded. "That's what I'm saying."

Enid looked at him in bafflement. "Like what? And what about our house? You love our house! That we created together. I *thought* we created it together. Every bit of it! Why did we spend all that time looking for the perfect fucking basket to put in the exact perfect place on the perfect restored barnwood shelf? *You're* the one who *insisted!*"

"Why are you so annoyed?" Hugo shrugged and leaned his head closer to Enid's. "Our house is great. I'm only saying that if Assembled Souls were choosing a décor for me alone, I would expect a lot more... animal heads on the walls. Animal skin rugs...tossed here and there." Hugo burst out laughing.

Enid hit him lightly on the arm, then hit him a second time for effect. "Oh my God, you're a horrible human being!" It was an expression the two of them had tossed back and forth for years. "Why am I even here? Why would I want *more time* with this horrible human beside me."

"Maybe I'm a little more nervous than I thought," Hugo said. "I am a little... punchy."

"A little," Enid said.

A large screen materialized out of nowhere on the wall in front of them, and on it, a woman of indeterminate age and background smiled at them. "Enid, Hugo, I'm Mayra. I will be your Caretaker throughout this process. Welcome to Assembled Souls, and thank you for taking the time to come in person. Of course, we could easily do all of this introductory work remotely, but we've found it to be so much more helpful to people this way. I hope that by the time your visit is complete, you will agree that it was time well spent."

Enid realized that she was nodding at the screen and whispered to Hugo, "Do you think she can 'see' us? I know they can hear."

"Yes, I can see you, Enid," Mayra said. "And see, right there, you're already demonstrating the usefulness of coming in person. I expect you will both have so many questions, and we've found that people are better able to think of them as well as feel comfortable enough to *ask* them when you're here with me."

Enid marveled at Mayra, who seemed to her a nearly perfect amalgamation. Mayra's shoulder-length, thick dark hair, eyes that seemed to shift between amber and brown, and mid-toned skin made it seem like her background could be any possible combination. She could believably pass for thirty-five, or fifty-five. Though Mayra was visible from the waist up only, sitting behind a beautiful oak desk like a newscaster, her body was very slightly overweight, a quality which added to both the authority and the warmth that she projected.

"The two of you will be interviewed separately for most of the time you're here today. But, while I have you together, we need to get your voice permission on a couple of the items that you also answered in your preliminary application. We always do this before we go any further, and we do it this way so that both of you can witness your partner's consent. All good so far?"

Enid nodded at the screen. Hugo gave a robust thumbs up while saying, "All good, Mayra. Shoot!"

"Do you give Assembled Souls permission to access and assemble your personal information, including, but not limited to, social media posts, data from smartwatches, electronic medical records, implanted medical devices, email accounts, video recordings, photographs, information stored on your cell phones and in your personal computers, and do you grant this permission dating back to the beginning of your electronic record and dating forward to the time of your death?"

"We do," Hugo and Enid replied.

Enid whispered to Hugo out the side of her mouth, "It's weirdly like we're getting married. Again."

"Do you agree to maintain the Assembled Souls Cube in your home and allow it to download and backup new data on its regular schedule until the time of your death?"

Again, Hugo and Enid responded in unison, and looked at one another. "You look bashful," Enid said, and she cupped his cheek in her hand.

"You look worried. No. Scared," Hugo said. He reached for her hand and gave it a long, tender squeeze.

"Thank you for those permissions," Mayra said. "Now, if you two are ready, let's get you into your separate rooms and get started. Have fun with this, you two. Most people find this really enjoyable."

Enid grabbed Hugo's hand. "I love you," she said.

"Enid," Hugo said. "We're not going to die *now*. We're just keeping options open for when we do."

4

"I apologize in advance if some of this seems tedious," the screen projection of Mayra said. "I mean, I know it's all stuff that you've answered before." Wow, Enid thought. Good use of slang and vernacular language. Very disarming.

"I was prepared to hate you," Enid said, then added, "I'm sorry. That just popped out."

Mayra laughed wholeheartedly and fiddled with the single strand of pearls around her neck. "Enid, I fully expect you to experience a wide, sometimes wholly unexpected, array of feelings about all of this. This is big stuff. Why wouldn't you hate me?" Mayra gave Enid a moment to regroup, then said, "Let's start with the boring stuff. Boring but important, OK?"

Enid noted the nuanced shifts in Mayra's facial expressions as she talked. She nodded. "I'd be a terrible friend to a blind person," Enid said. "As you can see, I mostly nod."

Mayra laughed again. "And those are exactly the kinds of things that make you *you*. The kinds of things we'll compile about Hugo to create *him*, not a duplicate, but *Hugo*." She paused for a moment again, looking into Enid's eyes to assess how she was faring. "OK, boring, important stuff. In the event of Hugo's death, you will have to activate your Cube. All you need to do is push the button, the green light on the bottom right side of the Cube. We cannot do this remotely; you need to push the button yourself as your final permission. Once the button confirms your fingerprint, the light will begin to blink instead of the solid green light you've seen all along, and you will know that the process of final assembly has begun."

"I understand," Enid said. "Hey, hold it. What if I'm not at home?"

"Good question," Mayra said. "You'll have a pocket fob that you'll need to carry with you at all times. All you have to do is activate your fob, and it will serve as your interim permission until you return home."

Enid nodded. "Seems awfully low-tech. Considering everything else."

"You're right," Mayra gave Enid a wry smile. "It's a nod to our legal department. They need that one final permission from you."

"That one final permission to recreate a human being. To recreate Hugo." Enid felt herself fighting back tears.

"You OK? Is there anything you'd like to ask or share with me?" Mayra asked. "Anything I can do, or do you just need a minute to sit with all this?"

"I don't know," Enid said. "It's… it's one thing to talk about this with Hugo, because of course, we do, we talk about these things, I mean, that's why we're here, right? Because we've talked about it. Rather endlessly, in fact. Everyone our age talks about this, this dying stuff. Well, not everyone, I suppose. Make a note for my avatar: Enid tends to talk in absolutes. I mean, plenty of people choose denial. And they choose it happily, as it turns out. I used to think those people were morons, but ha! Surprise! It's come to my attention that denial actually *works* for some people. It works brilliantly! It does! I'm babbling. That's not like me. I'm not a babbler, usually. But then this is hardly usual, is it? Make another note for my potential avatar: this is how Enid reacts when talking with a very lovely AI-generated 'caretaker' about the possibility of assembling an avatar of her beloved husband Hugo if he should meet his demise before she does. She becomes a babbler!"

"We don't like the word 'avatar.' We prefer not to use it," Mayra said. Enid wondered if she'd heard just a hint of irritation in Mayra's voice. Again, she thought: surprisingly human.

"Right! Assembled Soul! Forgot! Sorry!"

Mayra folded her hands atop her gorgeously aged oak desk and cleared her throat.

"You already knew everything I've said so far, Enid. You read it, and you signed it, and I would venture to say that you may have very nearly memorized it, because you're that kind of person. Thorough, and thoughtful, and… careful. Not cautious. Careful. You're also damn funny, in your own way."

"Did you already access my data?"

"No."

"You can tell all that because… you just can?"

"Yes," Mayra said. "It's true that I need to repeat those directions in person, but, more importantly, all that speechifying gives you some time to just… be here. Be *here,* in the sense of being surrounded by this possibility. You're right. It *is* entirely different than when you're in your own home thinking about Assembling a Soul, talking about it with Hugo." Mayra fiddled with a strand of her hair. She shifted in her seat. She very slightly puckered her lips every so often, just before she said something. Enid had been aware of these remarkably human gestures since the beginning of their conversation. And each time Mayra made one of these movements, it was slightly different.

"Were you Assembled from a living person, or are you an original creation?" Enid asked.

"Original creation."

"I figured," Enid said.

"You mean because I'm an idealized composite of Everywoman?" Mayra gave a droll smile.

"You have a sense of humor yourself," Enid replied.

"Thank you. We're proud of that. That particular trait proved much harder to achieve with Originals than with Assembled Souls. Oof, you wouldn't believe the clunkers some of my predecessors came up with thinking they were hilarious." She raised an eyebrow at Enid. "OK, the sense of humor thing is a great launch point to segue into some interesting things about Hugo as an Assembled Soul," Mayra said.

Enid took a sharp intake of breath. She released it slowly. "OK," Enid said. "OK."

"Ugh, that was probably a pretty abrupt transition on my part. I'm sorry. That was insensitive of me," Mayra said.

"I'm not sure there's a perfect segue into this particular subject, but I appreciate the apology."

"From here on, when I say 'Hugo,' I'll be referring to the Assembled Soul, and I'll be using he/him pronouns since that's how he's always identified. So. Hugo will be 97.87 percent exactly the same as the currently living person. In other words, there is virtual assurance that no situation will arise—ever—in your time with Hugo where you will perceive a difference in him. With the variety of data we will access, Hugo will look, talk, gesture, joke, make decisions and judgments just as he does now. He will have identical tastes, attitudes, perceptions, beliefs and fears. In other words, the whole of his personality will remain intact."

"Wow," Enid said. "Amazing. And more than a little frightening."

"The thing he will not have is memory. The technology has not yet arrived at a point where we can access or recreate a person's memories."

"Oh," Enid said. "Oh… I guess I knew that. It's a pretty hard one to wrap my head around. Aren't we mostly an assemblage of our memories by the time we're our age? Hugo's and mine. Isn't that who we are?"

"I understand what you're saying. You've lived long years and accumulated rich experiences, both separately and together. But you know what? This is where people in your age group actually have an advantage. I don't mean to be unkind, but… you're already in the process of navigating changes in your memory. Think about it. It probably happens on a pretty regular basis that you, or Hugo, or one of your friends, doesn't remember something that happened or that you talked about, even if it was pretty recent. You've been having to repeat things, probably more than you think."

"Ouch," Enid said. "Fair, but a tad harsh."

"Of course, the exception to the memory phenomenon," Mayra said, "is the electronic record. Anything that's been referred to in a text, or an email, or any photo or video clip that's on his phone or computer—Hugo will have those memories. They won't be the same as his memories now because they'll be limited to the specifics of whatever was recorded. But not so different, either. It will be sort of like Hugo has still shots from a movie, but he's never seen the whole film. He'll be able to infer and extrapolate quite a bit. But there will be gaps—unless you fill in the gaps for him. Does that make sense?"

"Kind of?" Enid said. "It's all pretty abstract."

"I can appreciate that," Mayra smiled warmly.

"Also," Enid wondered, hesitating, "this feels like… someone is explaining to me how my life, the life that I know, the life that I'm in right now, would mutate into science fiction at the push of a green button."

"I suppose how you feel about this depends a lot on how much you're using these types of technologies in your life now. For some people, this is not a particularly big stretch. For others, it's a giant leap. Anyway, like I was saying before, you have a leg up on the youngsters here. We've found the adjustment to the initial lack of memory to be far easier for you all."

"'Initial' lack of memory? Does it grow back or something?"

"Ha. No," Mayra chuckled. "It doesn't grow back, but it does stick. Meaning this: whenever you share a memory with Hugo, he will remember it from that point forward. It will become a part of him; he will not only remember you talking about the memory, but he will recall that memory as if it were one of his own."

"Wow," Enid said. "I guess that'll take a bit of getting used to."

"You're wise to understand that. All of this will take getting used to," Mayra said. "A lot of people are so eager to get their Soul up and running that they're just not prepared for *any* degree of adjustment. Hard as we try to prepare people, it doesn't sink in. Your attitude is quite realistic. It will serve you well."

"*If* I make the decision," Enid said. "The decision to do this."

"Yes. Of course. As long as we're on the subject of adjustments, would you like to talk about sex?" Mayra asked. "Totally up to you."

"Excuse me?"

"Would you like to have a conversation about the physical and sexual aspects of your relationship with Hugo? The Assembled Soul Hugo?"

"Um…"

"Again, we find that this works similarly to memory for people in your age range. Meaning, you've probably already been making… adjustments… along the way," Mayra said.

"Oh, that's a low blow," Enid said. "No innuendo intended."

"Haha, none taken," Mayra said. "I'm sure you know that people of all ages have been enjoying romantic and sexual relationships with AI companions for years now. There's been a ton of research and conversation about this, but not necessarily much that applies to AI 'recreations' of formerly living people—Assembled Souls. That's why I'm asking."

"Um, not to be coy, but if this Assembled Soul really is going to be Hugo, the *real* Hugo, then... I think we can figure it out. Him and me, I mean," Enid said. "Not you and me." It was a confident and witty front that Enid presented, but it was a front nonetheless. A pit arose in her stomach. She felt strangely shy, unready and unwilling to even consider a sexual relationship with an AI Hugo. What could that possibly feel like, she wondered. Wonderfully intimate? Like cheating? Enid didn't want to think about it. Not yet.

"Great," Mayra said. "There's also a ton of information that's included in your resource packet. If you find yourself wanting it at any point in the future." Mayra hesitated. She fiddled with a button on her suit jacket. "I don't want to offend you, Enid, but I feel like I want to address one... common misconception."

"Oh Kaaaaaaay," Enid answered.

"If you choose to have Hugo be born as a dense hologram, he will appear completely solid, except for an occasional shimmer along part of his skin surface, but he won't actually be *solid*. Meaning, he won't have parts of him that are, or can become, *hard*. Innuendo intended."

Enid blinked a number of times. Mayra fingered the button on her jacket.

"Are there actually people who believe that a hologram will be able to, well, that a hologram has a penis in the first place, a penis that can get an erection and..."

"Yes," Mayra said. "Lots of people. No joke."

"Well, I appreciate you setting the record straight on that. I could say 'no innuendo intended,' but I won't," Enid said.

"I believe you just did," Mayra said. She swiveled back and forth in her chair and arched her eyebrow at Enid. "All right then," Mayra said.

She shifted in her chair and looked into Enid's eyes. "That brings us to the last couple of things I have to cover from my end, then we'll take all the time we need to answer any questions, or address any concerns, from your end. Do you want to take a break? Can we get you some water, or coffee, or a light snack?"

"I feel like I'm on an airplane," Enid said. "Sorry. I use humor inappropriately when I'm... trying to appear calm while discussing life after my partner's death?... No, I'm OK. Press on."

"First, a reminder that you will have one year from the date of death to make a decision about beginning Hugo's Soul. I wish we could give more time, but we just can't retain the sheer amount of data for longer than that. We find that people generally find that time frame to be completely comfortable. Most folks make their decision well before the one-year anniversary date. We also require that you wait a minimum of thirty days to begin Hugo. We've worked hard to figure out the parameters that work best for *you*, and our understanding is that people need to get through the initial flurry of arrangements, and, of course, the initial grief, before your Soul can be truly beneficial to you."

"One year. I understand," Enid said.

"OK, we're down to the last couple of items. As you've read, you will ultimately need to make a decision about whether you would like Hugo to appear on a screen, just as I am now, or whether you would like him to be three-dimensional, appearing via what we call a 'Dense Hologram.' This is a very personal decision, and of course, there's no 'right' or 'wrong' choice. The biggest advantage of the screen Hugo is that he would be portable. You could take him literally anywhere you go, so long as there is connectivity. And some people just find that they're more comfortable with the screen because we're all so accustomed to that technology in our everyday lives.

"On the other hand, the Dense Hologram Hugo would be a life-sized entity, right there in the room with you. Hugo would talk and move and appear exactly as he does now, right down to the blemishes and creases on his skin—but only in the room where his portal is located. We have not yet advanced this technology to the point of portability. On the plus side, the portal will be able to generate backgrounds so the room you're in can appear as a favorite restaurant, a nearby park, a special place from your past, any place you provide photographs of.

"Of course, you want to take this decision seriously, but don't sweat it too much. You're choosing a starting point, really. You have the option of switching to the other form of Hugo any time within the first year. Again, Hugo won't think this is odd. He may even think it's kind of fun. But it's a one-time thing. You can switch forms once, but no ping-ponging back and forth after that.

"To help you think about this, I can appear to you now in my Hologram form, if you feel ready for that. What do you think?"

"I... uh... OK," Enid said.

The screen went dark, and Mayra appeared out of nowhere in the corner of the room. Enid instinctively drew back in her chair and raised a hand to her own cheek. Mayra walked across the room, clasped her hands in front of her, and stood next to Enid's chair.

"My God," said Enid. "You look quite a bit like Kamala Harris! That didn't come across so much on the screen." Enid scrutinized Mayra. Part of Enid felt suspicious, determined to find any possible chink in the artifice. Another part of her was entranced by the seamlessness of the illusion. "I think I'm about to start babbling again. This is quite... quite... overwhelming."

Mayra laughed. "I get that a lot. Not the overwhelming part, the Kamala part. She was one of the many, many faces that were used to create me. It's fascinatingly similar to genetics. Some traits exert more dominance." Mayra raised both shoulders and smiled at Enid.

Enid realized her mouth was open. "You have freckles! And a tiny little scar above your eyebrow!"

"And Hugo would have every one of his unique marks as well," Mayra said. "By the way, when we create an original, we offer people the chance to interact with their Original's Hologram—as well as with their screen—to help them make their decision. But—and you'll have to trust me on this—we've learned that it confused and unsettled people more than it helped when they were considering an Assembled Soul. It's no longer even an option. We don't fully Assemble the data until you push that green button on the Cube. There is no Assembled Hugo right now, lurking out there in the electronic ether. He will not be born until the human has ceased."

"Not be born…." Enid said.

"Enid." Mayra sounded so serious that Enid straightened up in her chair and put her feet flat on the floor. "I have one more thing to talk about. Do you prefer for me to stay in the room with you or go back onto the screen?"

"Um… your choice," Enid said.

"I spend more time on the screen," Mayra said. "It's a little more comfortable for me."

Mayra vanished from the room and reappeared on the screen. Enid blinked several times and said, "How do you do that?"

"I don't," Mayra said. "I'm not magic. Someone else has to implement the switch from one 'format' to another."

"Someone else is watching us?" Enid asked.

"Ha, no. It's AI. They're listening for sound cues. No different than Siri or any of the speech interpretation assistants that have been around forever." Mayra cleared her throat. "Anyway, this next thing is sort of like a hypothetical bundled up with a conjecture."

"You mean like a riddle wrapped in a mystery inside an enigma?" Enid said.

"Always good to throw in a Churchill quote," Mayra said. "I suppose. But, no, I meant that I want to address something that is highly unlikely, but important enough to cover while we're talking today. In the improbable event that you elect to bring Hugo back as an Assembled Soul, and that you ultimately decide you want to… discontinue his presence in your life… well, I cannot recommend strongly enough that you do *not* discuss this directly with Hugo. You can take my word for it, or I can point you to countless articles and pieces of research that confirm this generally ends in fairly tragic outcomes. And I don't use that word lightly, Enid. Truly tragic. For all concerned."

"Yikes," Enid said. "That sounds pretty intense. Do you think you can summarize without traumatizing me?"

"Let's just say that Hugo would enter into these conversations as if the two of you are discussing the idea of killing him. *You* killing him, I mean. Hugo will want to continue his existence, exactly like the living Hugo does." Mayra pursed her lips and narrowed her eyes. "Is that enough of a summary?"

Enid shrank down in her chair and cowered. "Jesus, yes. Yes." Enid sighed and looked around the room without really seeing it. "I'm sorry I asked," she said. "No, I needed to ask. I needed to. But I'm still sorry I did."

"That was the final issue I wanted to address before I turn you over to your interviewer," Mayra said.

"Wait, what? What do you mean, 'interviewer'?" Enid was puzzled. "What was this, if not an interview?"

"This was a conversation," Mayra said. "Your interviewer will be the one who asks you questions about yourself and takes you through a few psych tests and similar sorts of things. That's what I was referring to when I said you and Hugo should have fun with it. I didn't mean this conversation; this is pretty much all business, and some of it has been tough stuff. The fun part is next, where you get to play some games and talk about yourself."

"But I'd like *you* to interview me," Enid said. "I feel comfortable with you. I mean, holy cow, we've covered some territory here."

"You're right," Mayra agreed. "We have. And strange as this may seem, we've discovered that people are actually *more* comfortable when the interview is conducted with a different person—a stranger, if you will. Humans are just fascinating and quirky creatures, right?"

"Right. Make a note for my avatar. A note that Enid does not transition nor deal with unexpected surprises easily, and when such a curve ball is thrown at her, she gets flustered and peevish and does mean, testy things such as use the word 'avatar' even after the other… person… has made it clear that word is a big, fat no-no, and has also made it clear that she does *not* take *notes.*"

Mayra sighed and clasped her hands together. "I'm sorry. I clearly should have been more transparent about today's visit having two distinct parts that would be handled by two distinct... people. And by people, I mean—"

"I know what you mean. It's fine," Enid said. "I still think you look like Kamala Harris. Facial expressions, hand-clasping, and all. Always liked her quite a lot."

"I'm going to make a note of that," Mayra smiled. "Enid. Before I turn you over to your Interviewer, do you have any questions for me?"

Enid thought for a moment. Her voice was hushed, reverential, "Yes. I do," she said. "I've read about this, but I'm still confused. Will Hugo know that he's... a... an... Assembled Soul?"

"There's not a straightforward yes/no answer to that. Hugo will understand himself to be Hugo, because he *will be* Hugo. He will also understand that he is different than he was previously, but he will think about that much the same way as he thinks about his childhood self. The currently living Hugo knows that he was once smaller, that his voice was higher, that he had no beard. He also knows that he was born, and that he was a baby, and a toddler, and that he can't remember any of that! Hugo will think about himself in much the same way. He'll understand there's a difference, but it won't trouble him in any way, no more than it troubles him now that he's no longer a child with hairless armpits and no lines on his face."

"Could he be told outright? That he's an Assembled Soul? Or... can it be kept from him? Is there research or something about how that works out?"

"I suppose you would have to think about that with your own knowledge of Hugo. Your Assembled Soul Hugo would react to those possibilities just as your living husband would."

Enid looked down. It was a while before she spoke. "Can you feel things, Mayra?" Enid asked. "I mean, do you believe that you can actually *feel emotions?*"

Mayra looked thoughtful, and perhaps a bit wistful. "That's more of a philosophical question, Enid. And not one that I believe I'm capable of giving a definitive answer to. I'm made to have exactly the same responses that a living human being would have across an array of situations and experiences. Whether that translates into *feeling* genuine emotions, well, I'm not sure I can really know that about myself. I will add this, though. I exist exclusively in this space, as a Caretaker for the people who are considering Assembled Souls. I love my work, but I understand that the parameters of my space are limited. What I mean is, I have never had a person, a living human, who has loved me. I have often wondered what that would be like, how it might change me. I'm not able to predict what that might look like, but I know that it would. It would change me. Your love for Hugo will change him."

5

Enid burst through the door to the waiting room. Overflowing with a million things to say, the words, "Oh, my Lord, when was the last time you took an actual psych test—" were out of her mouth before she noticed anything in the room. A fire had been lit in the hearth, and it cast a sumptuous light on the walls and dark wood wainscotting. Hugo sat in a chair with his coat on, his head tilted back, gentle snores coming from his mouth.

"You're kidding!" Enid said. "You're able to just… fall sound asleep after all of *that!*"

Hugo jolted upright, rubbed one eye, and said, "Dear God! What in the world took you so long? Weren't we doing pretty much the exact same things? I'm relieved that we both lived long enough to meet up at least once again, even if just in the waiting area."

"That's not funny," Enid said. "Did you really finish so much sooner than I did? How's that possible? But, I mean, how would you even know how long it's been? You were snoring!"

"I can tell time when I'm sleeping," Hugo said. "You know that."

"Uh-huh, sure," Enid said. "OK, no cheating. Don't look. How much longer have I been gone than you were? What time do you think it is?" Skepticism dripped from Enid's voice.

"I finished just before 3. I would say it's… 4:02 now," Hugo said.

Enid pulled her phone out of her pocket, hit the button to check it, and quickly repocketed the device. "Damn, that's unsettling," she said.

"How can you still doubt me after all this time?"

Enid ignored his question. "Seriously, I felt like I was zipping right along through the chat with Mayra *and* the interview questions and psych tests and such."

"I took all the time I needed, my love. This is important. I'm hardly going to race through," Hugo said.

"Isn't Mayra sort of frighteningly likeable, by the way? I wanted to ask her out for coffee. It's weird," Enid said.

"She seemed great for the short time I saw her. I had a different Caretaker once we separated," Hugo said. "Clarence. Liked him!"

"What?" Enid said. "Really? I wonder why?"

"Well, Mayra can hardly be in two places at the same time," Hugo said.

Enid looked at Hugo in unconcealed disbelief. "Of course she can! She's an AI creation! She can be everywhere all at once!"

"I know that! But, Enid, these AIs are created to mimic humans. In every way. Mayra is designed to be just like a person. It's not like you're on ChatGPT, and Mayra has the whole cyberworld of knowledge at her fingertips. That's not human-like! Likewise, she can't be in two places at once!" Hugo remained quite matter-of-fact, Enid thought, if perhaps a tad too satisfied with himself.

"You've been studying," Enid said. She rubbed her hand up and down his arm and rested her head on his shoulder for a moment. "I do love you so. And aren't you absolutely dying with your coat on and that fire going?"

"Dying," Hugo said. "Let's get the hell out of here."

6

Hugo and Enid left the Assembled Souls building and walked past the picture-perfect garden without a word. Once in the car, Hugo reached for the audio controls then looked toward Enid. "What kind of music?" he asked.

She met his gaze, then looked down at her lap. "No music."

"Really?" Hugo paused. "That's highly unusual. For you," Enid said nothing.

The two of them stared out the front windshield for a good portion of the drive home.

Hugo cleared his throat and frowned.

"Yeeeesssss?" Enid said. You're thinking something?"

"Nope." Hugo scratched his nose and rearranged himself in the car seat. "Not really."

"Oh, very funny," said Enid. "I'm happy to ride along in silence, but you can't pretend you don't have any thoughts about... about... everything."

"My mind's kind of a blank," Hugo said.

"As if," Enid said. "You're a horrible human being."

"There's my girl," Hugo said.

They rode without speaking. Enid fiddled with her seatbelt buckle. She niggled at a speck on the dashboard with her fingernail. "Seriously, do you think we're making a mistake? Do you think this whole decision is a big, giant mistake?"

"We haven't decided anything." Hugo said. "Just like I said before we ever went in. We've arranged for a possibility. That's all. When the time comes, we'll have the option. But right now? We don't have to decide.

"When the time comes," Enid said.

"Yes."

"When one of us *dies*," Enid said.

Hugo gripped the steering wheel harder. "Yes. When one of us dies."

"So, you don't think that we've made a decision already? You don't think that doing all this is a… strong leaning in one direction?"

"No. We really don't need to have any idea what we may do until the time comes. When the time comes. Not right now."

"OK," Enid said. She glanced over and scanned Hugo's face.

He turned and gave her a purposefully fake smile. "You're overthinking."

"'I overthink the obvious when I'm alone," Enid said.

"Now you're quoting from songs," Hugo said. "And by the way, you're not alone."

"You're right. Thanks for reminding me. And for not being annoyed with me. Or are you? Annoyed with me?"

Hugo smiled. "Not that much."

Enid reached over and grazed her fingers along the steering wheel. "What do you think? Should we open a bottle of wine when we get home?"

Hugo knew what that meant. It was their private signal that the person who posed the question was interested in having sex. He looked over at Enid, intending to smile at her, but she continued to gaze straight ahead. Enid felt Hugo's gaze and realized her face was taut, her brow tensed. She made an effort to relax and was grateful that Hugo let it go.

"Of course," Hugo said. "Yes. By all means."

When they got home, Hugo wandered off to the bathroom to take his pill.

Even with the planning, the lack of passionate spontaneity, their love-making was urgent—breathless, groping, hunger for one another. And while they were usually playful, acknowledging the work-arounds of their assorted aches and pains and missteps with giggles and tender words, they were silent. Even their characteristic sounds remained muffled.

Hugo gripped Enid's shoulders tightly at the end. Great, heaving shudders ran through his body. Enid screamed out. A moment later, she went still. They both held their breath, aware that things felt different. Then, surprising both of them, Enid's tears came. Hugo stroked his finger along her cheeks to wipe the tears as they flowed, and as they subsided, he ran his fingers through her hair. Enid lifted Hugo's arm and slid her head into the crook of his shoulder. "You have to promise me something," she said.

"Of course, my love," Hugo said. "What is it?"

"You have to promise me that I can be the one to die first, and you can be the one who lives on."

Hugo lifted himself onto his elbow and looked directly at Enid. He cupped Enid's face between his two hands. Enid could feel the tension in his fingers. He kissed her forehead, tenderly, then kissed it a second time and lingered there.

"I need you to promise," Enid said. Her voice broke. "I really, really do."

Hugo pressed his forehead to hers and sighed.

7

Before they knew one another, neither Hugo nor Enid had thought of grocery shopping as anything more than a necessary evil. Hugo hadn't even bothered to get a shopping cart more than a handful of times, as far as he could recall, making do with quick visits to the deli counter for takeout. He found the long aisles and fluorescent lights and throngs of people staring at produce and cans and bags to be a sad and overwhelming experience. Enid simply found it boring. She had taken to having her groceries delivered as soon as she learned that such a thing was possible.

When the couple bought their new home, they ventured a trip to the nearby grocery store the night they moved in. Bone-weary from the move, they intended to make a quick trip, stocking up on a few necessities to tide them through the dreary unpacking that awaited them. Inside the entrance, Hugo and Enid felt it immediately. Their new neighborhood store was different. An unexpected warmth permeated the air. Hugo and Enid looked at one another. She laced her arm through his. They stood still, looking around, taking it in.

Bright color and delightful fragrance welcomed them. The floral display, positioned just inside the front doors, filled the air with the heady aroma of roses and lilies, mingling with the fresh green scent of foliage. The aisles were shorter, the lighting was softer, and as they took their first steps, a clerk nodded in greeting. And smiled! "Finding everything okay?" she asked, her voice warm and unhurried. Hugo and Enid exchanged a look—this wasn't what they had expected at all.

They spent more time in Candle Bros. Grocery that night than either one of them had ever spent in a store before. They walked slowly down each aisle, picking up items they would not normally notice as if they were rare and mystical treasures. Their imaginations ran wild with plans for future recipes, future dinner parties, a bounty of shared shopping trips and shared food.

Hugo and Enid had heard that Candle Bros. was renowned for its excellent, affordable wine selection. They lost all track of time while poring over rows of cabernets and pinot noirs, reading the staff's descriptions, comparing labels and vintages. A voice from right behind them made them jump. "Can I assist you with wine selection?" They turned to find a young man, eager and beaming. "I'm one of our buyers!"

"Ha!" Hugo said. "We're having the best time browsing. Thanks, but I think we're good." Hugo smiled at him and turned back to the wine.

"Well, maybe I can offer some ideas if you're having a hard time deciding," the young man said.

Hugo turned again, surprised that the clerk had pressed the point. Hugo took a quick look around and realized that he and Enid might be the last shoppers in the store. "Oh, lordy," Hugo blurted. "Are you getting ready to close? Have we been here that long?"

"In fact, yes." The clerk sounded apologetic. "In fact, we closed about ten minutes ago."

Hugo laughed heartily. "Enid, imagine that! New milestone for us. We've now been the closers at the *grocery store!* Who would have dreamed such a thing was possible?"

"It is truly a whole new world," Enid said. "Let's grab a bottle and raise a glass in our new home."

"Apologies," Hugo said to the clerk. "You should get out of here and go home. Pick a cabernet for us, if you would, and we'll skedaddle. I have a pretty strong feeling we'll be back here. A lot."

They were.

At first, their trips to Candle Bros. were driven by necessity—forgotten ingredients, last-minute cravings, the occasional impulse buy. But before long, they realized they didn't just *need* to go; they *wanted* to. Sunday shopping became a ritual, an easy pleasure they both looked forward to, whether they raced through the store in a hurry or wandered the aisles in unrushed leisure.

Early on, they got the idea to start their Sundays at the neighborhood café. Enid had a favorite muffin that she chose each week. Hugo, however, studied the pastry case as though it held the key to the universe, waiting for one to *speak* to him. Fueled by café lattes and sweet treats, they made their way to Candle Bros.

Over the years, their routine remained the same, though the store changed in small ways—the layout shifted, new employees replaced old ones, familiar products disappeared and reappeared. But the *feeling* of Candle Bros. stayed intact. It was still *their* place, their weekly reset, their quiet pleasure.

"Do you want to pick out the flowers?" Hugo asked.

Enid yanked a shopping cart from the corral and turned her head in the direction of the floral display. "You don't want to help pick them out?"

"Nah, go ahead," Hugo said. "I'll start the shopping. You can catch up."

"OK. Sure," she said. She began to push the cart over to Hugo, then frowned deeply and jangled it every which way. "God damn it, this cart is wobbly. I'm gonna get a different one."

"I can do it. Go ahead and look at the flowers," Hugo turned toward the cart corral.

"Don't get a wobbly one. They drive me nuts."

With his back still turned to Enid, he sighed loudly enough for her to easily hear. When he turned to face her, he ran his hand through his hair. "First, I'm perfectly capable of picking out a shopping cart. Second, do you have any idea what percentage of shopping carts you tend to find un-acceptable? Honestly, for *years* I worried that this was a thing with you. Your seeming *need* to find the first thing you chose completely… defi-cient. Like you always needed to *trade up* or something. I thought for the longest time that meant *my* days were numbered. Seriously!"

Enid kept an entirely straight face. "Do you realize how long we've been inside this store without getting more than twenty-five feet from the front door? Seriously."

Hugo raised one eyebrow and looked around the entrance. "Hey, what about an orchid?" Hugo said. When Enid looked at him blankly and did not respond, he continued. "What do you think about getting an orchid instead of flowers this week? Or both. I suppose we could get both."

Enid knit her brow in confusion. "We have an orchid."

"I meant one that's blooming. Flowers on it. Orchid flowers," Hugo said.

Enid's face fell, and she looked genuinely wounded. "I feel like you're giving up hope on the one we have."

"I'm not giving up hope," Hugo said. "But it's not blooming right now." Hugo made a shrugging gesture, intending to indicate this was no big deal.

"But it will! Remember how we ended up with all those orchid plants when we moved into the house? What was is—five different people got them for us as housewarming gifts? And every single one of them died except that *one*? But it never rebloomed. Five years. No sign of a bud!"

"I know."

Until that Brazilian woman said 'put her in the window.' Remember? She said 'her.' You have to do this to 'her' and do that to 'her,' and she will rebloom. And she freakin' did!"

"I remember!"

"You can't just give up hope. Not while there's possibility. You know. The old saying: 'where there's life, there's hope,'" Enid said.

"That's actually from the Bible," Hugo said.

"Really?" Funny. I thought it was from Anne Frank," Enid said.

"No, Anne Frank was the other way around: 'where there's hope, there's life'."

"The point is, all she needed—she, the orchid, not Anne Frank—was to be hidden from the sun, then put directly in the sun. We did that, and bang. She rebloomed. After *years!*"

"I wonder if the orchid felt a difference in you—how you treated it. Your thinking about it as 'her' and all."

"You're making fun of me," Enid said.

"Not really," Hugo said. "Well, OK, a little. But I'm also serious. Think about all the stuff we're learning about plants. Their awareness. How they communicate. It's mind-boggling."

"Agree. Let's do a little research when we get home. See the latest science on all this." Enid looked around and gave Hugo a playful tap on the butt. "*If* we ever get home. New record for us. We're still at the entrance."

"Well, it's not like there's a time limit," Hugo said. "I have all day. What about you? Any pressing things on your calendar?"

"No, but I *might* want to do something else on this particular Sunday, something other than shop. I'd like to have the possibility open, anyway."

"I thought you loved to shop," Hugo said. "I mean, not in general, you don't. You hate to shop. But you love our Sunday trip to the grocery store. Why, you hold the tradition as dear as how we decorate the Christmas tree and such things."

"See that woman checking out over there?" Enid said. "Second register? Bluish-purple coat?"

"Yeah, do you know her?" Hugo asked. "Want to say hi?"

"Don't know her," Enid said. "She came in the store at the same time we did. She was right in front of us."

"I see your point," Hugo said. "We can hurry along, if you're going to be insistent."

"I think we're light years away from the word 'hurry'."

"I'm going to get a new cart, and I'm going to pick out an orchid," Hugo said.

"Make sure it's a good cart.!" Enid winked at him.

Hugo raised both eyebrows dramatically at her. As he turned to get the cart, he did a little stagger step. Hugo winced slightly, and he placed his hand on his belly. He dropped it quickly when he saw that Enid was looking at him. She was clearly alarmed. "What's going on?" she asked. "What's happening?"

"Nothing much," Hugo said. "I'm just feeling tired. For no good reason."

"Why the hand on your stomach, then?"

"Wee bit of indigestion, I think." Hugo attempted a reassuring smile.

"Like I said, nothing much. Do think I'll lie down when we get home, though. Seems like a Sunday nap is most definitely called for."

"You say that as if a Sunday nap is an unusual thing. Isn't it always 'most definitely called for'?"

"True."

Hugo fussed when Enid said she would drive the short distance home, but she could tell his objection was weak, more a point of pride. Enid understood that he really didn't feel well, and she was worried.

Once home, Enid parked the car and said, "You go ahead in. I'll unload everything. It's not that much."

"Really?" Hugo asked, but he did not object. "OK, Cupcake," he said. "I suppose I can't argue with such resolve." Hugo got out of the car.

Enid opened the car window on Hugo's side. "Cupcake? Really?"

Hugo smiled at his wife, a big, warm one. He slapped his hand on the hood of the car, twice, the way they do in police dramas, and walked slowly toward the house. Enid watched him. Had that been sadness she'd seen in his eyes?

8

The entire expanse of fall gave the impression of being frail, dilute. The sun shone thinly, as if its rays were filtered through a murky window or a wet handkerchief. A combination of unusually warm days and lack of the usual rain kept the leaves from putting on their dazzling annual display. Instead, they paled, losing a slight degree of color each day, tending increasingly toward a dull brown.

As the colorless days paraded on, Enid had found herself adding an additional scoop of grounds to their morning coffee pots, putting fewer ice cubes into their regular glasses of bourbon, forgoing her sunglasses, leaning toward their windows—any number of small efforts to find some muscularity in the feeble days.

On one particular afternoon, toward the end of October, a breeze that had been light and soothing for much of the day turned angry. Trees shook and branches flailed. Leaves that had lost all remaining moisture, tethered to their branches by the merest threads, tore off the trees in great swirls, showering down all at once. Enid sat at the front window, transfixed, as symphonic whirls of grating and grinding leaves filled the air.

He will be peevish, Enid thought. He will be crabby until after dinner, at least.

Nonetheless, Enid was resolute that she must wake Hugo from his nap. He had to see this magical deluge.

Enid rose from her chair, the creak of its joints swallowed by the rush of wind outside. She tugged at the bottom of her cardigan, ran her hands slowly along the front, smoothing each wrinkle with undue care, such was the hypnotic draw of the downpour. With deep reluctance Enid stepped away from the window.

"Hugo," Enid called as she entered the hallway. She laughed aloud at how much her voice was swallowed into the ambient rush of weather, then put her hand over her mouth reflexively when she remembered that Hugo was napping, then laughed out loud once again when she realized she was on her way to awaken him. Enid hesitated outside their bedroom door. Steeling herself for Hugo's gentle pique, she prepared what she hoped was a disarming entrance. Enid pushed the door open dramatically while saying, "Once in a lifetime experience waiting for you, my darling!"

Hugo lay on the bed. His favorite nap blanket—the Mohair one they had chosen on their trip to Ireland whose fuzz shed everywhere and drove her nuts—was neatly tucked around him like a mummy. Enid had never stopped being both impressed and irritated by the depth of Hugo's slumber. Waking him was not easy nor did it happen without repeated attempts. But once the barrier of sleep had been breached, Hugo awakened in an instantly chipper and chirpy state. Unless he was awakened unexpectedly from his Sunday afternoon nap.

Enid made a raspberry sound with her mouth and took a few steps closer to the bed.

Enid noticed everything, all at once: the sound from her raspberry that hung in the air and made no echo; the expression on his face that looked as if Hugo himself had been drained out; his hand, his hand that held no life; some thickness in the room that consumed the noise of the outside storm.

Well before Enid reached for Hugo's cool hand, before she went to the end of the bed and jiggled his toe, then cupped his foot in her hand and held it, Enid knew.

9

Dear Hugo,

Do you have any idea how few people actually die in their sleep? And of that very small number, almost all of them die *at night,* not during a regular old afternoon nap on a random October day.

You've ruined October for me, ruined what used to be my favorite month of the year, even before I met you, even before I fell in love with a man whose birthday was October 7. And, speaking of things I'm pissed about, you just had to throw one more birthday in there, didn't you? One more special day where we drank a champagne toast to the day of your birth and marveled at the ever-so-slight daily changes we noticed in the colors of our favorite trees—a fraction of what we would normally see by your birthday, thanks to that warm, dry autumn. We took a walk and had to use our imaginations to detect any of the sharp, crisp smell of October as plants begin to dry and decay. But the wood fires, one of your very favorite smells—ah, we sniffed deeply at the scent of those, coming from so many chimneys as we strolled the neighborhood.

Thirteen days after that birthday, we had an astounding windstorm. The leaves tumbled down all at once, a blizzard of leaves, the likes of which I had never seen. I had to share it with you. I risked your annoyance at being awakened from a nap. But you did not wake up from that stupid afternoon nap that you took on October 20, and you never saw that leaf storm, and you never shared anything with me ever again.

Happy Birthday, my love.

I have thirteen days to decide.

Dear Hugo,

Time is almost up.

There are less than two weeks left to make this decision, and I don't feel like I'm even close to knowing which way to go, or even *how* to go about making this decision, without talking it through with you.

And that's just the thing, isn't it?

It's changed over the past eleven months. Of course, it has. It's less and less frequent that I make some discovery that immobilizes me, freezes me in place: finding your hidden toothbrush at the back of the kitchen drawer, the one you used if you stayed up into the wee hours, engrossed in one of your thrillers. You were afraid of waking me if you used our bathroom, afraid that the crazy gargle you insisted was necessary after a good brushing would jolt me into wakeful terror. Or unearthing your worn-out slippers way underneath the bed when I finally got around to fishing for dust bunnies. You know how much I hate that job. Or hitting a button accidentally on my phone and having your voice flood into my ears, an old voice message I'd kept. It's true that sometimes I would listen to some random voice mail—I would choose to. I might even listen over and over. I'm not even going to tell you how many times; it's none of your business. You can't imagine how different it is to *choose* this, as opposed to having your voice, *you,* shoot into my brain unexpectedly.

Anyway, you get the idea. I could avoid going through your closet and your drawers and all of your spaces as much as I wanted to, but still, again and again, these unexpected pieces of you kept emerging, kept reminding me that I was not one bit farther along in letting go of you than I was on the day you died.

I love writing letters to you.

Dear Hugo,

Every once in a while—not as often as I might wish, I'm afraid—the solitude feels wonderful. Those airtight windows in the TV room that you insisted on really do the trick. That room is a vault of silence. No sound. No sign whatsoever of a world outside that room. I like to imagine that I enter it from some place far away, that I've chosen this room where the silence immerses me. It thrills me. It allows me to float on it, and it embraces me at the same time. It makes me think of that Christmas. You knew how much I dreaded the long, bleak stretch of winter after the holidays were all packed up and put away. You bought me that book about Hygge, all the different ways those clever, clever Danish combat the cold darkness. We turned off all the lights and lit a million candles and ran around the apartment shouting "HOO-gahhhhhh! HOO-gahhhhhh!" to one another once we figured out how to pronounce it. That may have been the hardest we ever laughed.

It is an ecstasy of memory. I am filled with lightness, as if all those candles are inside of me and I really could float away.

But here is the thing. The time always comes, always, always, when I want to leave the room. I want to find you. I want to tell you about this. *You.*

Dear Hugo,

There is a gaping hole in me, deep in my core. I feel it, all the time, some absence of myself. Sometimes I catch myself lifting my shirt, looking down at my belly. I half expect to find a real hole, a six-inch circle that I can see right through. I am confused by the solid abdomen that I see.

There are times when I fear that the size of this hole, this absence of any substance whatsoever, has grown so large that I will implode. My body will curl into itself, and shrivel, and get sucked into this absence until I am entirely gone.

How am I supposed to make a decision, especially such a monumental one, when I carry this hole?

Dear Hugo,

We met one another too late in our journey to have children. And though we talked again and again about what that experience may have been like for us, it was never an option. I managed, despite rather endless stupidity before I knew you, to never get pregnant. I never knew if that was something my body would be able to do—carry a human life and birth it into the world. I feel now like I imagine I would have felt if we'd met earlier, if we'd wanted to have children, and found that we couldn't. *I* couldn't. I think I would feel the barrenness. Feel it physically. Like the part of my body that is essential to human life didn't work the way it was meant to work, and I would actually *feel* this. I would sense a defect, an organic part of me that is, to use one of your very favorite words, catawampus. I feel barren now. This hole, this flaw, this terrible absence is you. Of course, it's you.

OK, blah blah blah, I think I've talked to you enough about the hole. I haven't told you about the other side.

And oh, believe me, I can hear you saying, when you hear this, that I am talking out of both sides of my mouth. That I'm contradicting myself. I'm going to say the same thing that I've always said to this: people are complicated. We are allowed to have different and conflicting feelings at the same time. It means we're deep.

This one's harder to explain.

Sometimes there is so much feeling inside of me, even with the hole of nothingness, I fear my body can no longer contain it. It's too big, too gargantuan, to be confined. My skin is going to burst apart. I am about to explode into a billion particles of bone shards and gore and, if there is such a thing, soul.

I panic. I try to breathe. I even try to imagine that the hole inside me is growing, and that it can swallow up some of this overwhelming pain, this missing of you that is too large to stay inside.

I hate you. I'm not just saying this. I truly hate you. I have never known hate before. I know now that I had never felt this before, because I feel it now. Right now, I feel it. Hate. It's ugly and it's dark and it's a million cliches. It has a taste. A slightly salty, disgustingly metallic, putrid taste that wells up all the way from my bowels through my stomach and into my mouth. It's shit. It's my shit. My shit of hate.

You died. You fucking *died,* Hugo.

You lying, fucking, bastard, motherfucker. You promised. You *promised* I could be the first to die.

Dear Hugo,

Want to know one of my very favorite memories? When we went to the Florida Keys. My one and only time there. You wanted to show me all the places your family went every year when you were a kid. You even wanted to eat at the same restaurants and have me try the dishes you remembered and loved from decades before. We joked that we would commit to eating key lime pie at least once every day, and breakfast was a perfectly acceptable time for pie. You confessed that you'd always wanted to rent a convertible at least once in your life, and you were embarrassed about this—*really* embarrassed. You kept changing your mind and saying, "Never mind. It's stupid. Let's not." But I insisted. And we got to the airport in Miami and picked up that giant, crazy, shiny white convertible. You were *so* happy. You got into that driver's seat, and your face just totally relaxed into this... smile. It wasn't your mouth; it was your whole face. I'd never seen it before. Serene and excited at the same time. And you backed out of the parking space, shifted the car into Drive, and said "Yeah, baby, now we're living." You reached out your arm to put it around my shoulder. Except you miscalculated. You punched me right in the face. Right square on the cheekbone.

You slammed on the brakes, looked at me in horrified shock, and I looked back at you in horrified shock, then I burst into laughter. And you burst into laughter, interrupted every few seconds by a profuse apology. I mean, you apologized so much that I had to insist that you stop, or I was gonna get seriously pissed off.

We took that trip for your sixtieth birthday. We sat on a glider in a seaside restaurant that you had sat on every year from the time you were eight until you went away to college.

I made you a book from all the photos we took on that trip, but we never once looked at it.

It sat on the shelf, and neither one of us ever brought it down to look. It was as if there were an unspoken understanding between us to let our memories of that magical trip remain inside of us. We talked about that trip to the Keys. Often, we talked.

I wonder now. Did we have some feeling, some instinct, that bringing the past into the present like that—looking at pictures from a time that was gone—would... rearrange our memory, interfere with it in some way that was bad?

Is that what I would be doing if I brought you back?

Dear Hugo,

The minute I stepped outside for my morning walk, I could hear it. A steady roar filled the air, and it was coming from the lake—more than two blocks away! I hurried over, imagining the entire time what I would see. The sky was a deep, steely gray, an unusually wintry look for the beginning of October, with a colossal wind that was not unlike the day that you died.

Sure enough, enormous gray-black waves arose and broke everywhere, some of them pounding against the rocks in shooting sprays and others bursting randomly into a foamy, crazy, haphazard, thunderous symphony.

Because the nights have been so cold, blocks of ice have already formed on the lakefront rocks. And because the wind and waves have been pounding as well, the ice formations have grown impressively. I still hate winter, but you know how much I love this one part. You know that this is why I get up so early in the morning, why I don layer upon layer of armament against the weather—so I might see the sun rise over the lake, so I can gauge the minute changes each and every day: the patterns in the sand, the detritus on the beach, and, as winter progresses, the continual evolution of ice formations. Later will come stalactites and caves, and ultimately, ice mountains that look like extraterrestrial landscapes.

But this morning, this early October morning, so much earlier in the year than usual, here is what I see. At the exact moment I pause at a midway point along the rock wall of the lakefront, a wave that I did not see coming crashes into the shore right where I stand. A boulder of ice tears off from the force and plummets into the lake, sending up an enormous spray, as if a whale has just breeched directly in front of me. It is breathtaking. It has literally taken my breath away. And my head is spinning, thinking about the nature of time, and coincidence, and all the little circumstances that led to me standing at that spot at that exact time and seeing that... wonder.

And then I think. Who can I share this with? Who can I tell this to? And of course, there are people I could tell. There are many people. I could text them, or call them, and I could tell them about this. But I don't. I won't. This is the kind of thing that I tell to you. It's too small, and too monumental, and too intimate, and too... I don't know... everything, to tell anyone but you.

I'm rereading Stephen Hawking. In honor of our thinking—perhaps tongue in cheek and perhaps not—that *A Brief History of Time* contained all wisdom. How very often one of us said to the other, "Remember to look up at the stars and not down at your feet." It was practically our mantra. Do you remember the next part? "Try to make sense of what you see and wonder about what makes the universe exist."

I wonder if I have done much of anything else since October 20 of last year.

So, back to yesterday's small miracle, the fleeting moment of the ice block shearing off and crashing into the lake. A moment that arose from an endless string of random coincidences. A moment that came and went, as ephemeral a point in time as all points in time are. I know this. I've felt the truth of this in my very bones since my brother ran into our usually empty dead-end street to catch a baseball. He scrambled out of our front yard with his eye on that high fly ball at the exact moment that Mrs. Leonard backed out of her driveway at exactly the right speed and hit his leg at exactly the right angle to send him aloft at exactly the right arc that he landed on the asphalt and broke his neck and died.

I'm losing my train of thought.

My point is that I know how accidental, and how fleeting, every moment of our lives is.

I also know that, when you were here, everything felt different. You were the person who reminded me to look up at the stars, yes, but you were also the person who was *there*.

We were the witnesses to one another's lives, and somehow, that gave a weight, and a bulk, and a significance to things.

I feel as if I turn to you a hundred times a day, literally turn my body to tell you something, only to find myself with my mouth hanging open in an empty room.

Dear Hugo,

I read a lot about grief. And loneliness as well. There is so much out there. We are a terribly lonely world.

I read that it helped a great number of people to talk to their "deceased loved one" (ugh! What a phrase!) as if they were still there. I tried it for a period. I actually carried the urn with your ashes from room to room with me. Sometimes I would talk to it (you?). Sometimes I would just set it down in a place where I could look at it whenever I glanced up. I got one of those necklaces that contained a smidgen of your ashes, and I wore it all the time. I fingered it at random times. Occasionally, I whispered to it. One time, I held it against my cheek and kissed it.

In the end, I felt like an idiot. Maybe even pathetic. I took the necklace off one night and never put it back on. I returned your ashes to their special place on the shelf we spent so much time looking for.

None of it made me feel like you were *here*, like I had *you* in any real kind of way, any way that helped me bear your absence.

I also read that talking to yourself can be helpful. Don't think about it as if you're talking to some imaginary (or DEAD) person, all these articles said. Just talk to yourself! Be your own enjoyable companion! Well, I've always thought that talking to yourself out loud was highly odd. I mean, what's wrong with having one's thoughts remain in one's own head? Why would we need to hear our lone little voice echoing around an empty room? But I strive to be an open-minded person. That Big-5 personality test that we both had to take as part of the Assembled Souls interview process confirmed that I am highly open to new experiences, so I decided to give it a go. (Remember? I asked you what secret truths your Big-5 had revealed, and you said, "Why in the world would I read about myself? I'm *me*." And I said, "Why in the world wouldn't you? It's *fun*!" And you said, "Fun? I'd rather stab my eyes out.")

I lasted less than one day. The first time I spoke out loud to myself, I burst out laughing. The second time, I cried. Felt even more pathetic talking to myself than when I was pretending to talk to you. And there's the word: pretending.

Every single thing that I've tried to feel your presence has smacked me upside the head with an overwhelming feeling of pretending. And every single thing I've tried to help grieve you, to accept that you are really, truly gone, and that I must confine you to my memories and gradually bear the indescribable magnitude of this loss—nothing has helped. Nothing.

Dear Hugo,

Well, wait 'til you hear this one, this crazy tale of how your wife, in her agony of grief and indecision and moral quandary and anguish and, did I mention grief and agony, and a general dwindling down of time and days and hours to make a decision about whether to, whether to, open the door to your tomb and let you appear to me. I decided I should seek counsel. More counsel. I should get all the wise and thoughtful input that I could (even though I've gotten quite a lot over the past eleven-plus months, rest assured about that, and I believe you would say: too much). And in a stunning illustration of circularity born of utter desperation and despair, I thought: why not seek advice about whether to bring my deceased husband back into my life through the wonders of AI... well, why not seek counsel from, ta-da, AI!! I am well aware that I undoubtedly sound deeply unhinged right now, but I assure you that I had nothing but the most clear-eyed and sincere intent when I posed the situation to my good buddy ChatGPT. Turns out my buddy had a very great deal to say, and rather than try to summarize and paraphrase, I'm going to share the entirety of their... thoughts.

Fasten your seat belt, Hurley.

Hello, Enid,

First, let me say I'm sorry for your loss. Grieving is one of the hardest and most complex journeys we undertake as humans, and your contemplation of bringing Hugo back through an Assembled Soul reflects just how deeply you cared for him. It's a profound decision, and it's natural to feel conflicted.

The possibility of recreating Hugo with such accuracy is remarkable and raises new questions that touch on love, identity, and the nature of relationships. Let's explore these together:

1. What Are You Seeking From This Experience?

• Ask yourself: What do you hope to gain from having Hugo's Assembled Soul in your life? Is it comfort, closure, companionship, or simply the feeling of his presence again?
• Assembled Souls can be extraordinary at recreating the behaviors, voice, and even emotional responses of a loved one. But they are, at their core, a reflection of what's been programmed into them, drawn from data and patterns. While they might evoke Hugo's essence, they cannot fully *be* Hugo.

2. What Does "Recreated" Really Mean?

• Even if this new version of Hugo feels indistinguishable from the man you knew, it's a reconstruction—a product of technology, not biology or soul.
• Ask yourself: Does it matter to you whether this recreated Hugo is truly autonomous or just emulating what he would have done? If the experience feels authentic, that might be enough for you—but understanding this distinction could shape how you approach this new relationship.

3. Can This Technology Coexist With Your Grief?

• Grieving is a process that helps us honor the past while learning to live in the present. Introducing an Assembled Soul may complicate this journey.
• Some find comfort in the familiarity of such technology, but it can prolong feelings of loss or create an illusion of resolution that feels untrue.

4. Will This Change How You Remember Hugo?

• Memories are deeply personal, and they're often colored by time and emotion. Reintroducing Hugo in a "living" form might alter your relationship with those memories.

• For example, will you be able to reconcile the static memories of the Hugo you lost with the evolving nature of the new version? This could bring comfort but might also introduce tension as the new Hugo begins to differ in subtle ways from the man you knew.

5. How Will This Affect Your Own Growth?

• Relationships evolve over time, and loss—while painful—often shapes us in profound ways. Bringing Hugo back might pause some of that personal evolution.
• If you recreate him, will you feel free to grow in your own direction, or might his presence keep you tethered to the past?

6. The Meaning of Love in This Context

• Love often transcends logic—it's about connection, memory, and shared experiences. This recreation could allow you to continue expressing love, but it might also raise questions: Is your love for this Hugo the same as it was for the original?
• The depth of your feelings might remain unchanged, but the context of this relationship is fundamentally different. Acknowledging this difference could help you navigate any complex emotions that arise.
• Longevity and Control: Does this recreation have limits? Can it evolve beyond the Hugo you knew, or would it remain as he was when he died? Understanding these boundaries could help you set realistic expectations.

Enid, recreating Hugo with such precision is a deeply personal decision. It could provide immense comfort and a sense of continuity in your life. But it's also important to acknowledge that this recreated Hugo, no matter how lifelike, will never fully be the man you loved—it will be a new version, one shaped by technology and limited by what it knows of him.

That said, if having this version of Hugo brings you joy and helps you honor his memory in a meaningful way, then perhaps it's a gift worth embracing. Just remember: your love for him isn't diminished by the choices you make now. It endures, whether or not you decide to bring him back.

Warmly,

ChatGPT

That completely did me in. Like the stupid old saying goes: stick a fork in me, I'm done.

But it also helped me to decide. I've decided.

When I went off to first grade, way back in the days when kindergarten was just a few hours in the morning, school was the first time I'd been away from my mother. This was before my brother died, and things were safe and good, and my childhood was everything it was supposed to be. Still, I had such a hard time falling asleep many nights. Other nights, I would fall asleep from sheer little kid exhaustion, but I would awaken later and find myself watching the dot patterns that my eyes or brain or something generated in the darkened room. I wouldn't be able to fall back asleep, hard as I tried, and I would call for my mother. I remember her coming in and sitting on the edge of my bed, snuggling up against my little body and asking me what was wrong. "I'm gone from you for so long now," I would say. "Sometimes, I just need to see you. I need to see your face. Not just in my mind. Right in front of me. I just need to see you."

That is where I am. I don't want to get caught up any further in all of those biggest questions of all time about love and existence and memory and longing and grief, nor do I want to embroil myself in the biggest questions of our time, about the gaping loneliness of our world, about how much we turn to technology to fill our voids.

I just want to see your face. Right in front of me.

10

Enid read numerous accounts of different people's first reunion with their Assembled Soul. She poured over descriptions of how they had chosen the location, and the time, and what they would talk about. She dove into information about how to prepare for meeting the person whom she had known intimately and loved deeply in their new form, after the passage of time, carrying the pain of their absence. She knew she was driving herself crazy trying to determine the best possible situation to reunite with Hugo. Hugo would have thoroughly disapproved. He would believe she was overthinking. He would be hurt that Enid put so much effort into managing the circumstances rather than trusting the strength of the bond between them.

Still, it mattered to Enid. She had chosen to revive Hugo in the Dense Holograph form. She would set him up in their den. It was not their largest room nor the room with the expanse of windows where she had watched the storm of leaves nearly a year prior. It was the room where they had their morning coffee and where they often sat in the evenings to chat or read or sip their bourbon. One entire wall was comprised of bookshelves the two of them had cobbled together from old barnwood. Enid had always felt those shelves held the truest spirit of their marriage. The bottommost shelf held books that dated back to Hugo's childhood as well as his parents'. On the next shelf up, Enid's own history was similarly represented by her own and her family's most beloved stories. The remaining shelves held a mixture of the favorite books that Enid and Hugo had read and shared during their years together as well as a hodgepodge of their pasts—fossils from a beach they'd strolled in Ireland, stones from a vacation in Michigan, a drawing that Enid's mother had made when she was a teenager, a tiny rusty farm tractor that had been part of the display under Hugo's Christmas tree. Her childhood copy of *The Little Engine that Could* displayed next to Hugo's childhood copy of *The Velveteen Rabbit*.

Enid had largely avoided the den since Hugo's death, generally limiting her time there to a monthly cleaning. She ran the vacuum, dusted the surfaces. She visited with the objects on the shelves and allowed their memories to pour into her. Yes, this was the room where she wanted to spend the most time with Hugo, but the room felt different after her decision had been made. Enid picked up the fossil from the Irish beach and fingered its cool, smooth surface. Hugo would remember this; she had taken a million photos that day and shared them to Hugo's phone. The Michigan stones would mean nothing to him, as they had left their phones in the car for that particular hike. Enid felt her body tense as she rearranged the little stones to dust the shelf underneath them. She blinked back tears as she ran her fingers along the frayed, stained cover of *Velveteen Rabbit*. The book that Hugo had treasured for decades would be meaningless to him.

The decision to have Hugo reside in their library/den/TV room still didn't settle the matter of where to have their first meeting. Because of Hugo's ability to generate backgrounds, Enid continued to fret, bouncing among her three favorite options. Much of Enid loved the idea of greeting Hugo in the den itself, the room in their home that was comfortable and familiar and intimate. Enid well understood that Hugo would not experience the layer upon layer of shared memories that the room contained, but she also knew that a great deal of it was undoubtledly contained in Hugo's electronic record—photos, video clips, and the like. Perhaps it would comfort her, she thought, if she set out tea in his favorite cup, even if it would mean nothing to him. Or perhaps not? Would that be too jarring of a start—Hugo quickly demonstrating the parts of him that were missing? He would not be able to pick up the cup. Nor would he be able to drink from it.

The park bench where the two of them frequently met in the late afternoons seemed another good possibility for a first meeting. They both loved the outdoors in general, and their neighborhood in particular. They had gotten in the habit of arranging to meet at a particular bench on days when they were both out of the house late in the day. They loved to watch the changing light, sometimes talking and sometimes sitting silently. At the inevitable point that one or the other of them expressed ravenous hunger, they walked home. The park bench backdrop would provide familiarity, Enid thought, but without the minefield of missing memories contained in the den.

Their favorite restaurant was the third alternative Enid weighed. Enid loved everything about it, and Hugo loved how much Enid loved everything about it. With its towering timbered ceiling, exposed brick, artfully peeling plaster, sculptural arrangement of industrial pendant lights and mismatched furniture in the lounge area, Enid often joked that they had seen her coming, and that she was prepared to move in and live there in a heartbeat. Enid and Hugo had been there so many times—probably once a month or more for *years*—that all of their individual dinners blended together into a giant amalgam of the restaurant Square. Enid felt certain that Hugo's electronic record of Square was extensive and would afford him an overall "memory" of the place. At the very least, he would know that it was big and loud and relaxed and fun.

In keeping with her lifelong pattern, Enid took a great deal of time to contemplate the options, creating endless scenarios and imagined conversations in her mind. One morning, Enid reached for the bar of soap during her morning shower and said, "Bingo." A resolute decision had congealed at that moment, for reasons she herself did not fully understand. Nonetheless, she knew with certainty she wanted her first conversation with Hugo to happen in their den. He would be in his place on their couch, and she would be in hers. She would activate him, then enter the room with their steaming teacups, and Hugo would be waiting.

11

Enid chose an utterly ordinary moment to contain the event she imagined would be the most monumental of her life. She decided to set the scene as if Hugo had just awakened from his nap. Enid wasn't pretending, nor was she in denial. She simply didn't know where else to begin.

Enid peeked around the corner for her first glimpse of Hugo. She braced herself for something to feel off—a stiff posture, an odd smoothness to his skin, a slight hesitation in his movements. But there he was, familiar in his every unique imperfection: the sloping of his shoulder, the haphazard part of his hair, the crease along his earlobe.

Hugo sat at his usual spot on the couch in his usual position—sitting at an angle so he would be facing Enid when she sat down, one arm lying atop the back of the sofa, one knee resting on the sofa cushion. With his back turned, Hugo could not see Enid and could not know how long she stood there. Enid felt herself trembling and thanked the universe that she had opted to put their tea in mugs rather than teacups. The rattling of the cups in their saucers would surely have gotten Hugo's attention. He would have turned, and she would not have had this time to collect herself, or at least to try. Enid took long, deep breaths to slow her heart. She felt it pounding, racing. She pushed down fear that it may beat its way right into her throat.

Hugo wore his lightweight burgundy sweater and an old pair of jeans. His outfit, at least, was not a surprise. Enid had chosen it. She took a final deep breath and entered the den.

"Oh. There you are," Hugo said.

Enid parroted, "There *you* are." She set down the cups, folded her hands in her lap, unfolded them and placed them at her sides, trying to appear natural.

"I wasn't sure where you were," Hugo said. "I'm not exactly sure how long I've been up. From my nap."

"From your nap," Enid said.

"Right," Hugo said. "Did I miss anything?"

"During your nap." It was a statement. "Right. Some leaves blowing around," Enid said. "Blowing around rather dramatically. I actually tried to wake you."

"You did?" Hugo said.

"I did," Enid said. "But..."

"But you were afraid I'd be a cranky ass, so you changed your mind," Hugo said.

"Yes!" Enid struggled to match Hugo's tone. Everything about him was easygoing, natural.

"As a result, here I sit, right as rain, in fine fiddle," he said.

"In fine fettle," Enid said.

"What?" Hugo said.

"In fine *fettle.*"

"What the hell does that mean?"

"I don't know," Enid said. "But that's the expression: in fine fettle."

"Ridiculous!" Hugo said. "What in the world is a 'fettle'?"

Enid erupted in laughter. A crack had broken through the dam inside of her, and relief poured through. Hugo, this Hugo who sat beside her on the couch and scratched his chin and wiggled his knee and knit his brow and flicked his hand when he said the word "ridiculous" was so entirely, wholly, fully, utterly her husband. He was perfectly Hugo. A shudder went through her. And then another.

"I'm glad you're getting such a good laugh at my expense," Hugo said. "At my not knowing the word 'fettle.' If there even *is* such a word. I wouldn't put it past you to make up a word then laugh at me for not knowing a word that you made up in the first place. Or maybe you're laughing at me for blindly believing your made-up word. Either way, you're a horrible human being."

It was an expression they had used frequently: "you're a horrible human being." Enid was undone by how normal everything seemed. And how *quickly*. So normal that it was surreal. All of the hours and days and months since Hugo lay down for his nap. All of that time, that infinitude of unbearable time, where he was gone and she was left in an agony of trying to sort through the wreckage and tatters of her own mind. It vanished. Hugo, her Hugo, sat in front of her. Enid became lightheaded. She saw Hugo and the room as overly bright, the details in sharp focus.

Hugo crossed his arms in pretend pique. Enid laughed. How strange, she thought, that the words "you're a horrible human being" could have the effect they did, could make her feel so connected, understood. She instinctively reached for him. She needed to touch her husband. Enid expected the buttery soft cashmere of his sweater beneath her fingertips. Something wasn't right. The fabric was too smooth, too uniform, like a surface of plastic. Enid drew her hand back as if she'd been scalded. The surface of his sweater wavered and shimmered for a few seconds before appearing solid again. Hugo had not noticed. Enid gasped, her eyes riveted to his arm.

"Jesus, what's wrong? Why are you staring at my *arm?*"

Enid shifted her gaze, fixing her focus on a specific item on their bookshelf—her mother's drawing—trying to ground herself. "Nothing," Enid said. "I'm OK." But when she looked back at Hugo to offer him a reassuring smile, she felt nausea gathering inside. She covered her mouth with her hand and barely made it into the adjoining bathroom before being overcome with retching. She heard Hugo calling out from the den. Then, she heard his voice coming from just outside the bathroom door. There had been no sound of footsteps to announce his approach.

"Be out in a minute," Enid said. "Sorry. Sorry for the sudden departure." Enid knelt on the bathroom floor, her head hovering over the toilet bowl, waiting until she was sure her body had nothing more to expel.

Enid stood, splashed cold water on her face, rinsed her mouth out, and gazed at her image in the mirror. I look just like myself, Enid thought.

How can that possibly be? Mayra's words from their long-ago conversation resurfaced in her thoughts. *Hugo will understand himself to be Hugo, because he will be Hugo.* She flushed the toilet a second time, rinsed out the sink bowl, and cleared her throat several times. She considered Mayra's words again before returning to the den. Hugo looked at her expectantly. "I'm sorry," she said. She cleared her throat and wiped the back of her hand against her mouth. "Sorry. About that," she said again. Enid remained standing. She looked at the floor and clasped her hands awkwardly in front of her.

"Why are you apologizing? You're *sick.* Tell me what you need."

"I think I needed just that," Enid said. "You asking me what I need. That feels like... like the exact right thing." Enid sat down and sighed—a long, audible sigh. She kept a safe distance from Hugo to ensure that she would not disrupt his surface again. "You lay down to take a nap. There really was an amazing storm. I'd never seen anything like it." She turned and looked into Hugo's eyes. "I did try to wake you. I wanted so much for you to see it."

"Sorry you couldn't wake me," Hugo said. "That's weird."

Enid rushed to switch subjects. "The weather's changed now. It's gotten really cold."

"Are you feeling better?" Hugo asked. "You're looking a little better."

"Definitely," Enid said. "Getting there." Enid knew there would be an adjustment. It's an expected part of the whole process, she thought. Nothing more. It's really my Hugo.

12

Enid's head spun. She contemplated her first day with Hugo as she went about her nighttime routine. Everything felt like a miracle, like a God that Enid never fully believed in had reached into Enid's life and touched her with the magic of a true second chance. Enid pictured her husband lying dead, on their bed, wrapped up like a mummy in a fuzzy blanket. She saw that the man she loved had ceased to be. And yet, here he was. When Enid left Hugo in the den, he had been sauntering casually around the room, browsing the bookshelves, looking out the window. She wondered momentarily about what, exactly, went on inside of him when he was alone, then thought, no, never mind, that's too much to think about right now.

Enid knew it was not strictly necessary to put Hugo into Hibernation Mode when she went to bed at night; it was an option. Enid liked the idea that Hugo could "sleep" at night while she did. She found it comforting—they could essentially go to bed and wake up at the same time, just as they always had. She had mulled over the two options for Hibernation: one in which all of Hugo's functions would shut down, but he would remain Visible, and one in which his Dense Hologram form would vanish until he was reawakened—Invisible.

Enid didn't expect the choice to be a big deal, nothing compared to having Hugo back in the first place. Still, everything was brand new, and she found herself tiptoeing into the den after she put Hugo into the Visible Hibernation mode. Hugo sat on the sofa, both feet flat on the floor, his hands resting atop his thighs, his back erect. His face looked relaxed, almost as if some of the fine lines and creases of age had smoothed out just a little. He stared straight ahead, his eyes dull and focused on nothing.

Enid watched him for a while, then she carefully took a seat on the sofa. "Hugo?" She spoke quietly, tentatively, then waited. There was no response. She leaned her head closer to him and said, louder this time, "Hugo?" Nothing. She snapped her fingers in front of his face and was immediately horrified that she had done so. "Oh my God," she said to Hugo, "I've turned you into some sort of parlor trick! This is just too weird! I can't handle you being here, but not being here!" She raced over to switch his Hibernation Mode to Invisible. Hugo vanished.

Enid returned to the couch and sat again. She ran her hand back and forth along the spot where Hugo had been sitting. "This isn't so perfect either." She spoke to the air where Hugo's face had been. "You just got here. I don't like not being able to see you." Tears streamed down Enid's cheeks. "But you *did* get here. You did."

13

Enid opened her eyes the next morning and smiled into the dark. "Good morning," she said aloud. "I am not talking to myself. I am talking to my *husband*." She relished the words, the sound of them as they rolled off her tongue, the movement of her lips as they released the words into the dark. The buoyancy of her energy needed an outlet. She grabbed the extra pillow that lay beside her and hugged it.

Everything was different. Again. But in the most magnificent way.

14

The smile on her face. Enid felt it as she put her arm through her cozy robe. She recognized the lightness in her step as she made her way into the kitchen to start her morning coffee.

We have a full day ahead of us! Her thoughts swirled. *Our first full day.*

We can do anything we want. Anything!

Enid stopped in her tracks when she realized she had dumped a fifth scoop of coffee beans into the grinder—enough for a full pot. Enough for two people to share. She chuckled at herself, feeling even more buoyant. Hugo's reborn presence was brand new, but already, he was slipping back into her routines, her reflexes. She was making coffee for him. Their old habits felt like muscle memory—they were coming right back.

Enid reached for her favorite mug as the coffee brewed. She reached for Hugo's. *Hold your horses, Enid,* she thought. You *need to think this through.*

When Hugo had been alive, Enid made their morning pot of coffee. She loved the ritual of it, and she loved the progression of sounds—the metal scoop diving into the canister of beans, the beans clanking into the grinder, the whirr of the grinder, the burbling when she poured the cool water into the pot's tank. Hugo had long given up suggesting they take turns. He believed in doing his fair share, but he well understood the simple joy the coffee making brought Enid.

Hugo would take his time to get out of bed. He would yawn, stretch, and make his way into the den. His particular pleasure was perusing the morning news, making mental notes of various things he wanted to discuss with Enid. When he heard the obnoxious beep that announced the coffee was brewed, he knew Enid would arrive momentarily, bearing their fresh, full mugs.

That was the routine. Right up until the day he died.

Will Hugo remember this?

Enid considered.

Hugo could not drink coffee. If she came into the den with only one mug, would he notice? Would he piece it together—right away on day one? Realize what *he* was?

She could not bear the possibility.

Enid placed both hands on the kitchen counter and leaned forward as if asking it to support the weight she carried inside. "OK," she said aloud. She leaned harder, then pushed away and stood straight. Then again, louder, "OK."

Enid reminded herself that she could activate and deactivate Hugo whenever she chose.

She would finish her coffee in the kitchen. Then she'd activate him, go into the den, and spend time with her husband. She savored that thought and ran it through her head again.

What about reading the news? Will he remember that?

As Enid finished her coffee, her body hummed with the sense of possibility. But there was another side as well. An unease. *What else have I forgotten to prepare for?*

She rinsed her mug and placed it carefully in the sink. No reason to rush, she told herself. But her body moved with a quiet urgency, an underlying quiver, the way she felt decades ago before a first date or the rare times she had to speak in public.

The den remained dim, though morning light had begun to creep in. A muted, blue-gray glow crept across Hugo's side of the couch and the end table holding his tablet. Enid stood still for a moment, letting the quiet settle around her. Was it her imagination, she wondered, that the air felt different? Expectant?

Enid had placed the discreet Assembled Souls console just outside the den. From where she stood, she'd be behind the couch when Hugo appeared, able to see him without being seen. She thought she might need that moment.

Enid took a deep breath and pushed the activation button. She had seen this before—when Mayra appeared out of thin air during Enid's first trip to Assembled Souls—but it was no less jarring. And no less miraculous.

Hugo appeared instantly. No whirr of machinery, no flickering.

There he was. Sitting on the couch in his usual spot. He scratched his nose. He cleared his throat. He reached his arm to rest it on the back of the sofa, and when he did, he saw Enid. "Morning, Hurley," he said.

"Morning," she replied softly. "Hurley." He remembered the nickname they called one another. It took her by surprise. "Hurley" was not an everyday thing. They used the name randomly and sparingly. *It must have been somewhere in his record. Still…*

"Looks like you've already had your coffee." Hugo smiled at her and patted the seat beside him on the couch.

Enid blinked. She hadn't said a word about coffee. He couldn't smell it. He couldn't have heard her making it. He'd been deactivated. She smiled back, but she felt unsettled. She was wandering blind through wholly uncharted territory, groping her way along.

She looked at Hugo, trying to anchor herself. "Cat got your tongue?" he asked, teasing.

Enid felt her anger rise. *Get it together, girl. You knew this would take some time to get used to. Don't get stuck in your own bullshit.* Hugo *is* here. *Don't waste a minute.*

"Nah," Enid said. "I have plenty to say. Even since last night."

Hugo nodded. "I would hope so. You always do."

Enid sat beside him, drinking in the lines on his face, the crease on his earlobe that had deepened to mark the passage of their time.

There *was* so much to say, but for now, it was enough to sit beside her husband, again, even if the edges of it all still trembled.

15

Enid was deeply protective of Hugo. She approached her time with him as if he may die again and she would be left alone a second time. She also recognized that their long partnership had been interwoven with the presence of others—a rich friend group they both cherished. Dinners filled with laughter. Days spent hiking or at the beach. Shared vacations. The ongoing rhythm of planning, reliving, and recounting every get-together.

Enid wanted to begin including friends in her time with Hugo, but the thought filled her with dread. She worried that someone might say something that could alert Hugo to his… status. She worried they'd treat him like a science experiment, prodding and poking to gauge his responses. She particularly fretted that they might challenge his memory, or lack of memory, in ways that would unsettle everyone involved. Worst of all, someone might touch Hugo—accidentally or not—and cause the solid-looking man to transform into a quivering, wavering mess.

Enid found that her friends fell neatly into one of two categories—those she thought of as the cyber-curious and the other camp that she labelled the cyber-phobic. Maddie and Ivy had been begging to meet Hugo since Enid first told them of her decision. Junie and Hazel were mortified at the choice she had made to bring Hugo back. They were terrified that he may somehow go rogue, murder Enid in her sleep, and take over the world.

The decision made itself when Enid got a message from her friend MJ one morning. MJ and Hank had been their closest couple friends for years, and their divorce had felt like a death—one that had drawn Enid and Hugo closer in their shared grief. MJ had moved across the country, remarried, and built a life. Hank and his friendship had drifted away. But Enid and MJ had stayed in touch, and now, MJ was coming to visit.

It felt right that one of their oldest friends should be the first to meet Hugo.

But how to prepare him? How to make this first encounter feel natural when nothing about it was?

Maybe, Enid thought, she wouldn't explain it at all. Maybe she could just tell him a story.

16

"You want to hear something strange?" Enid said. "There was a period of time, probably a few months or more, when every time I drove past MJ and Hank's old house, I got teary. I never told you about this. Every time! I couldn't figure it out. I thought and thought about it. Then, one day, I was driving past their house, and I felt the tears, as usual, and this picture just popped into my head. The four of us—you and me and MJ and Hank sitting around the butcher block in their kitchen, howling with laughter. Fall-off-our-chairs, obscenely loud, snorting, tears-streaming, pee-in-your-pants laughter."

"I'm not remembering this," Hugo said. "Say more."

"They had just finished remodeling their kitchen, and they called us up one evening, totally last-minute, and asked if we were free to come over right then. We just assumed they were thrilled about their new kitchen and wanted us to see it. It was finally *done*—I mean, my *God,* it had taken for-ever and claimed large parts of their sanity. But it turned out, that wasn't it at all. They were beside themselves about having created a new appetizer. They couldn't wait for us to try it! So we drove over there, and they met us at the door and walked us into the kitchen, keeping up this giddy, chatty banter the whole time, going on and on about how amazing and delicious it was. And so easy! So, they ushered into their brand-new kitchen—that they were completely ignoring—and had us sit down around their cus-tom-made butcher block that they were also completely ignoring. There was a platter in the center of the butcher block with all these different types of crackers and corn chips. They kept saying, "Are you ready? Are you ready?" Then, very ceremoniously and with this sudden, reverential silence, MJ set a plate on the tabletop, Hank unwrapped a brick of cream cheese and tossed it on the plate, then MJ opened a jar of salsa and poured the whole jar over the brick of cream cheese. That was it! That was the miraculous invention! They were virtually bouncing up and down, saying, 'Wait'll you taste it!'"

"Well, you and I must have looked at them with... I don't know... utter blank bewilderment. Their faces fell, and they stood there stock still. It was like all four of us had been frozen on the spot. We looked at them, and they looked at us, all four of us in this stunned silence, and at the exact same moment, the *exact* same moment, all of us started laughing, and we couldn't stop. We kept laughing and laughing and laughing. I couldn't tell you a damn thing about what their new kitchen looked like—Lord, this was decades ago—and I don't remember anything whatsoever about how the miracle appetizer tasted, but I will never forget that laughter. It felt like the four of us were in some sort of perfect moment.

"They were *such* good friends." Enid paused. She moved a little closer to Hugo. "You held me so tight when we found out they were divorcing. So tight. It wasn't so very many years after that appetizer night...

"Anyway, that's why I was getting tearful every time I drove past their old house for all those months. That's what was bubbling around inside of me.

"That was one of the happiest times of our lives. Four people—all at once—we got swept up in something magical."

"I love it when you tell me stories about us," Hugo said.

"Do you?" Enid said.

"Oh, God, yes," Hugo said. "Your voice. Your expressions as you tell the story. The story itself." Hugo paused. "Too much? Am I making you self-conscious?"

Enid laughed. "No, I don't think so. I think I'm good."

"Well, what about the other side?" Hugo wondered. "Maybe all this flattery on my part is causing your head to swell. Before we know it, your enormous head won't be able to fit in this room!"

Enid laughed. "You never could resist ruining the moment, you dog." This is what Enid had wanted: Hugo listening, laughing, teasing. Exactly this. But when she looked at him, she caught the furrow on his brow. "Baby, I was joking! I was teasing you!"

"Oh, I know. It's not that," Hugo said. "'One of the happiest times of our lives.' It's just that… are you saying you were happier then, *we* were happier then, than we are now?"

Enid was taken aback. Hugo seemed to be reflecting. He seemed to be *feeling doubt*. "No, I'm not saying that. Just a memory. A part of our life together, that I wanted to share. Relive. With the person who was there with me at the time."

"Keep those stories coming, I say," Hugo's familiar, easy tone buoyed her.

"We were a whole lot *younger*," Enid said. "A *whole* lot. But if we weren't so damn old now, and so much time hadn't gone by, well, the memory wouldn't be quite so precious." Enid paused. She swatted away the inclination to reach for his hand. "And I wouldn't need to share it with you quite so much."

17

"So you can't *go* anywhere with him, right? MJ asked.

"Right," Enid said. "We're just here. In the den. That's the deal with the Dense Hologram."

"How'd you decide?" MJ wondered. "I mean, I've started to see more and more people who clearly have the portable version. They're all over the place. Every time I do some work in a coffee house, or when Tim and I go out to dinner, you see people sitting at tables alone, yakking away with their screen."

"It was rough. The decision," Enid said.

"I've heard there's a controversy brewing about whether 'companions' are going to have to buy their own seats when they go to the movies or a concert or whatever. Cause, you know, a lot of people still want to go to stuff with their partner," MJ said. "So they can share it and talk about it afterward. Like they used to. I mean, sheesh. How do you decide that? Is your AI more like a baby on an airplane—you hold them on your lap the whole time, so they get in for free? Or should they pay full adult price because they're the recreation of a full adult?" When MJ looked over, Enid's face looked tense, and her eyes were cast down to the floor. "Sorry, I'm getting lost in the weeds here. I do want to know how you decided."

"It was hard! Part of me wanted to be one of those people like you're talking about. I thought, if I'm gonna bring him back, I want to go EVERYWHERE with him. Each and every one of our old favorite places! And take long drives! And hikes! And stay in charming little towns! And…

go and do whatever in the world we want." Enid's voice petered out. She looked tired.

"But…"

"But?" Enid continued, "Well, for starters, I'm self-conscious."

MJ laughed.

"OK," Enid said, "not in general. But I am in this particular way. I really am. I realized that every single person who saw me with a portable Hugo would *immediately* know something very very deeply personal about my life—I had lost someone and brought them back. That just seemed weird and creepy and sad. I'm an old white woman. I've never had the experience of people taking one look at me and making assumptions and conjectures at the very first glance, let alone know something that was actually *true*.

Plus, I started thinking about how much of Hugo's and my time outside of this house was spent basically eating food and drinking either coffee or wine. Two things a screen Hugo would *not* be able to do. So how much fun was it going to be to drag him all over the damn world and then either eat alone, so he wouldn't be 'there' in the first place, or have him with me while I *described* food that he was watching *me* eat? Hugo and I used to love going to wineries all over the place, or even local restaurants, and doing wine tastings. I started having nightmares of desperately trying to describe wines to a screen Hugo—'high tannins! A little funk in the glass! Cigar box! Leather and dark chocolate!' Very, VERY weird and creepy and sad."

"Wow. This stuff gets crazy-making, doesn't it?"

"Yes." Enid paused a second and repeated, her voice quieter, "Yes." It was MJ's turn to look at the floor. "I'll tell you what's crazy-making," Enid continued. "Crazy-making is when you find yourself at the very last thread of your very last rope, when your time to make a decision about whether to bring Hugo back is very nearly up, and you find yourself turning to ChatGPT to ask its advice."

"I would normally think you were being witty, but I doubt that's the case right now."

"Nope," Enid replied. "No, I am definitely not being witty. Now that

I brought it up, I don't really want to get into all that. I was in a total slump of despair." Enid shrugged. "Truth be told, it was actually kind of helpful. Asking Chat, I mean. Except it signed its message to me 'Warmly, ChatGPT.' I thought that was...." Enid's voice trailed off. She closed her eyes and shook her head back and forth.

MJ's mouth dropped open just a bit. "Do you know how exceptionally weird this all sounds? Asking AI to help you make a decision about AI?" MJ shook her head back and forth as if to clear her thoughts. "I'm sorry," she continued. "I feel like I'm being insensitive. Every bit of this...well... it all sounds ridiculously difficult. ALL of it. Jesus, Enid."

"Well, funny enough, haha, it did help me decide. The chat with Chat, I mean. It got so cosmic and existential and philosophical, and in other ways, so utterly granular, that I ended up feeling like, fuck it. Fuck all of this. I need to see Hugo. I *need* to. And not on a screen; I needed the 3-D dense hologram, even if we are forever confined to the den. He will be life-sized. And solid. Hugo will be with me."

18

"Does it feel like him?" MJ asked. "I mean, do you feel like it... he... is really Hugo?" MJ set down her mug and looked at Enid.

"I do." Enid added, "I mean, I knew what I'd read and heard and watched on reels, but when your very own life partner is right there, right there in front of you—a year after he's *died*—and he's sitting the same way and saying the exact same things that you know Hugo would say, and making all the little movements and gestures and twitches...." Enid's voice got quieter. "He has the same weird crease on his earlobe." An image of Hugo's sweatered arm warbling and shimmering when she'd grazed it flashed through her mind. She looked away, avoiding meeting MJ's eyes. Enid turned to glance out the window. "You know, I was sitting right here. On this couch. Watching the most amazing blizzard of leaves swirling every which way. I went to wake Hugo up from his nap so he could see it." She met MJ's gaze. "Yes, it feels like I have Hugo back. He's really here."

MJ took a long swig and looked thoughtful. "Enid, I gotta tell you. I can't even begin to think about making a decision like this one. Can't even begin."

Enid nodded. She cleared her throat and nodded again. "We haven't gone anywhere yet," Enid said. "I mean, we can't really go anywhere, like we said, but you know Hugo can generate backgrounds, right? He can make the den look like other places, any other place, really, as long as it's in his memory. Or if I show him a picture. He can do that, too. We could sit on a bench along the Seine or atop a mountain in Glacier National Park.

I haven't tried it yet. Thought I'd start small—the park bench right here in our neighborhood. The one where we'd meet up lots of afternoons."

"But you'll really be right here at home? In the den?"

"Yep. Like I said, I haven't tried it out yet. Guess I'm a little nervous. About taking the next step in our relationship." Enid laughed nervously.

MJ did not join her laughter. She rearranged herself on the sofa and leaned forward. "Well, that gets into something I really don't understand. If Hugo is generating backgrounds and stuff, doesn't *he* understand that he's not the human Hugo? Doesn't he get that he's… something else?"

"When I asked Mayra—my caretaker at Assembled Souls—that very question, she said there wasn't a straightforward yes or no answer to that." Enid looked in MJ's direction with a weary half-smile.

"What's that supposed to mean?" MJ rolled her eyes and released an exasperated sound. "What the hell are you supposed to do with *that?*"

"She said that Hugo would think that he's Hugo, and that he'll understand that he's different. Both."

MJ shot a look at her, MJ's expression moving from frustration to concern as she glimpsed the complicated mix of feelings that Enid's face belied.

The two women sat in silence.

"I think… I think right now, everything is new. I have Hugo back." Enid cleared her throat and fiddled with a piece of fuzz on the sofa cushion. "I couldn't get used to it, MJ. I'm not just talking about the grief, either. Grief so consuming it eats every fiber of your body and worms into every thought in your head and every microsecond of every day. Still, it was more than that. Different. *I* was different. It's like I… I just wasn't able to be myself in the world. Not without him. My own footsteps were just too loud, too pointless, without his presence."

"Not to switch the subject, and I fully acknowledge that you've always made great coffee," MJ said. "But I say it's time to switch to wine."

Enid laughed, a genuine belly laugh. "You're a true visionary, or maybe a mind reader, or something."

Enid scooped up the coffee mugs and returned a few moments later with an open bottle and two wine glasses. "I hope red is OK," Enid said. "I only have red these days. But don't worry. At least I have lots of it."

It was MJ's turn to laugh. "As well you should."

Enid poured, handed one of the glasses to MJ, and reached for her own. MJ raised her glass. "Cheers," MJ said. "To... new frontiers."

Enid clinked her glass against MJ's and continued to hold it up. "You know, one of my very favorite things to do is admire the color of red wines—they're exquisite! The subtle differences in the hues. The remarkable variation from one to another." Enid wagged her head from side to side as she said, "Rust. Ruby. Garnet—" Enid laughed heartily. "Now it's my turn to be lost in the weeds. But it's true. It's a small but mighty pleasure of mine."

"Mmmm."

"Hugo may not be able to taste the wine itself, but he can admire the colors with me like nobody's business," Enid said.

MJ gave her a sidelong glance.

"Back to your question about Hugo," Enid said. "About whether he 'understands' that he's an AI recreation." Enid paused and looked thoughtful. "At some point, he'll understand."

"What do you mean?"

"Sooner or later, some glitch or something will slip through. A glitch that Hugo notices. And when that happens, the data will tell Hugo the truth. Apparently, it won't bother him. That's what Mayra said."

"It won't bother him? He's AI. Does anything actually 'bother' him?'"

Enid ignored the question. "But, I don't know." Enid rubbed her forehead with her thumb and index finger. She took a healthy swig from her glass. "I don't want our time together to turn into some endless discussion where we talk about *it*—what happened, how I made my decision, how long he was gone. I just want to be with him now, in the present. You know?"

MJ leaned forward on the couch, her eyes wide. "I'm trying," she said.

"I suppose I'm trying to put that off as long as I can," Enid said. "I lived my life without him for a year, and now he's back. I want to hang out. Him and me. Have a chance to say all those little things that bounced around inside of me. Listen to him laugh. Watch him hike up the waist of his pants before he sits down. Watch him wiggle his belt around when he stands up."

"Are you saying you're trying to keep it from him?" MJ said. "You're purposely trying to keep him from knowing?"

"I suppose you could say that."

MJ nodded her head and looked thoughtful. "Allrighty then. Is there anything else I should know? Before I meet him?" She picked up her glass and took a long drink of her wine. "I'm sorry if I sound unsupportive or disapproving. I really don't mean to be. This is big, and mind-boggling, and… completely new to me. I'm just trying to catch up. With this new world."

"Believe me, I know," Enid said. "I really do."

"The wine helps. But there's not enough wine to…" MJ's voice drifted off.

"…To make it seem possible that this is all one life, the same life where you and Hank and Hugo and I were young and laughed all the time and couldn't have even begun to imagine this… possibility."

"Well put," MJ said. "OK, then. Let's go. Ready as I'll ever be to meet Hugo."

"Try to act natural."

"Yeah, that is a pretty crazy thing to say under the circumstances." MJ's expression was wry, and mournful.

"Oh, one other thing," Enid added. "Don't touch him. Just… don't."

19

Enid walked back into the den and plopped down on the couch. "God, I miss her. I SO wish she still lived here."

"Is she all right, Enid?" Hugo looked deeply concerned.

"MJ?" Even though Enid had settled herself on the couch at an ideal point between close enough and not too close, she inched slightly farther away.

"She looks *so* different, so many deep lines in her face," Hugo said.

Hugo's statement baffled Enid. "What are you talking about? She looks *great.*"

"You honestly thought so?" Hugo asked. "I was pretty taken aback, to tell you the truth. I felt like I was resisting the urge to ask her if something was really *wrong.*"

"Wow, I really thought she looked terrific. She—" The realization hit Enid. Hugo's visual image of MJ was likely years, maybe even decades, old. Over the many years since MJ had moved thousands of miles away, she visited regularly. But when she visited, she raced around to connect with a lot of her old friends. And once Hank was no longer in the picture, MJ and Enid met for breakfast or coffee or drinks, outside of Enid's house and without Hugo. Typically MJ would come in at some point and give Hugo a quick, warm hug. But no one took pictures. There would be nothing recent for Hugo's "memory" to access.

Hugo's image of MJ wasn't just outdated—it was stuck.

"Oh, God," Enid winced. She hoped Hugo hadn't seen it. "I'm sorry.

This is my fault! I didn't think about how long it's been since you actually saw MJ—in person. She and I always scoot off somewhere when she visits. I can't even think how long it's probably been. No wonder you're... kind of freaked out."

Enid laughed, but it did not sound authentic.

Hugo looked thoughtful. "Am I seeming freaked out? Do you think I seemed weird to MJ? God, I'd hate to think I made her uncomfortable."

"No," Enid said. "Really. No, not at all! I'm sure she didn't notice anything unusual." Enid forced a small smile, knowing that MJ noticed everything, every bit of it unusual. "Don't worry about it. You were great. I know MJ was really glad to spend some time with you." Enid imagined that, by now, MJ had arrived back at the place where she and Tim were staying. MJ would be recounting her afternoon with Enid and Hugo. Enid tried to picture it. But as long and well as they had known one another, she could scarcely imagine what MJ might be saying about her experience with Enid's reassembled husband.

20

"Hey, I was thinking maybe we could meet at the park later," Enid said. "Are you tired?" She looked at Hugo. "After MJ's visit?"

Enid knew that Hugo wasn't tired, that it wasn't possible for Hugo to be tired. But it's exactly what she would have asked him. She would have known that MJ's visit had left Hugo with a drowsy satisfaction, replenished by human connection but a little weary.

Enid was amazed at how easily she had slipped right back into their long-ingrained ways, how they anticipated each other, how they said the same things they always had.

"No," Hugo said. He ran his hands through his hair, glanced at them, then placed them in his lap. "Not tired at all. It's good to see folks. Really good. Fresh blood." He rubbed his hands together briskly in pretend glee, stared at them for a second.

"Well, then, what do you think about the park?" Enid asked. "You up for it?"

"Absolutely," Hugo said. "Name the time; I'm there."

"Let me get some stuff done, and let's say… four? See you there?"

"You betcha."

Enid caught herself beginning to gasp and pretended a cough to hide it. "You betcha" was another of Hugo's signature phrases. Enid stood up quickly and turned her head away so Hugo would not see her eyes filling.

21

A thrill went through Enid. She felt buoyant, elated. She had not known what to expect, but this was light years beyond her imagination.

Stray leaves swirled through the air as she approached the park bench. She watched in amazement as the leaves skittered across the pavement and made scraping sounds. Birds sang from the branches of the trees, occasionally flying from one to another, sometimes landing near Enid's feet and pecking around.

She looked up from a sparrow's playful hopping to see Hugo approaching the bench from the other direction. He walked with his head down, as if protecting himself from the wind. His hands were thrust deeply in his trench coat pockets. When he brought them out to pull the coat collar up around his neck, he saw Enid and smiled. "Colder than I thought it would be," Hugo said. "I'm freezing already."

"We're in the *park!*" Enid spread her arms wide. "We're really *here!*"

"What an exceptionally odd thing to say, Enid," Hugo said. "Since we agreed to meet *at the park*."

Enid tilted her head back and laughed with genuine, unfettered ease. "I know. I'm just so happy to be here."

Hugo brushed his hands across the shoulders of his coat, as if to brush away wandering leaves that may have landed there, then gave a visible shiver.

Enid's face abruptly shifted. "Can we sit for a while?" Her voice held concern, slight confusion, and a degree of unwelcome wariness. "Are you too cold?"

"No, let's sit. For a little while," he said.

Hugo sat and patted the space next to him. Enid joined him and let out an audible "Ahhhh." She shielded her eyes from the sun with one hand and looked around. It was November, just past the height of fall color. But their favorite bench happened to be surrounded by soaring locust trees whose small leaves turned brilliant yellow, transforming them into towers of a million tiny flames. Enid had always loved the late afternoon sun of autumn. It had a thick, golden richness that she looked forward to all year. The sumptuous sunlight filtering through the yellow leaves made the whole world glow. "Oh my God," Enid said. "Will you look at that *light!*"

"Breathtaking," Hugo said. "Truly and utterly."

"I don't think I used to notice light very much," Enid said. "Now I notice it all the time. Patterns on walls that the sun makes coming through windows. Reflections on sidewalks and parked cars—all kinds of surfaces I see when I'm walking." Enid chuckled. "Sometimes I take pictures. Well, not sometimes. Pretty much all the time. I give myself one day to look at them. I look at them over and over for that one day, then I delete them."

"Really?" Hugo asked. "Why delete them?"

"I don't know. I guess I don't want to be that crazy old lady who died with a million pictures of light patterns stored in her phone."

The word had come out of her mouth before she could stop it—died. Enid felt her body tense. She jerked her head to see Hugo's reaction, but he was casually looking around.

"Hmm." Hugo turned toward Enid, smiled and shrugged one shoulder. "Pictures on your phone, or no pictures, it's possible that the 'crazy old lady' ship has already sailed."

"Haha, very funny."

"Seriously, though," Hugo continued. "This sounds wonderful—your own personal study of light. You should keep them. The pictures." This felt exactly like what Enid had wanted, what she had been unable to live without. Her and Hugo. Together. Telling him what she had noticed, what she was thinking as she went about living her everyday life. Listening as he did the same.

"Look at the patterns the sun is making right now, the shifting mosaic of shadows, all around us. This is the kind of thing I believe I will remember all my life."

"And I will, too," Hugo said. "Drink it in, my love, because I fear I underdressed and am damn near frostbitten over here. Let's get home before gangrene sets in."

"OK," Enid said.

Enid knew that Hugo had always been vulnerable to cold, even more so as he had gotten older. But they were in the den of their own home. It was seventy degrees.

She also knew that locusts are among the first trees to lose their stunning leaves in the fall. In the actual park near their house, the locusts had long been bare.

22

"I wish I hadn't been so cold," Hugo said. "It was a glorious day."

"It really was," Enid said. "Hmmm…" Enid looked dreamy, wistful. "But you know what? I can't ever decide if fall is my most favorite time in the park, or if it's spring," Enid said.

"Why decide? Why not have both be your favorite?"

"It's so *you* to be so practical like that," Enid said. "And the answer is: because. Because I have an emotional, sentimental attachment to the idea of favorites. They help me know who I am, and they keep me from feeling wishy-washy."

"Ah. Well, in that case…" Hugo gave her an impish grin. "I can't stand the thought of you feeling wishy-washy. But, hold it. Why spring? What's spring got going for it that could rival a day like today? Those little leaves lit up like a legion of matchsticks."

"Why spring? What do you mean 'why spring? 'Well, because of the tulips, of course."

"Tulips?" Hugo asked.

"Yes, Mr. Spacely, Mr. Space Cadet, tuli—"

With Enid's dread of winter, its endless days of gray and cold, she clung to every modicum she could find that heralded the coming spring. Mere minutes of increased light each day after the winter solstice. Birds' songs becoming more and more robust. The magical day when the first tentative green shoots of new plants poked their way through the snow.

And the one that she and Hugo shared—the tulips.

They had made a ritual of watching them together, from the first sign of their clumped leaves to the growth of their slender stems, to the tight green flower buds, to the dazzling flowers. They had memorized the park's tulip beds. They knew exactly where the earliest bloomers appeared, and where the mid-season tulips followed shortly behind. When the leaves of the early bloomers had faded to a yellowish green and the flowers had fallen into petals on the ground, the tall, late-season tulips came into their own. They loved the entire array of colors and types, but red was their shared favorite.

A flash of memory struck Enid—Hugo's sweater, the way it had shimmered and flickered and melted. The perfect metaphor for how she felt.

Tulips had been a passion.

Hugo did not remember.

23

A chilled glass of her favorite rosé in hand, Enid turned the corner toward the den. At the threshold, she was greeted by the sound of gentle waves rolling onto the shore. The shrill keows of gulls. *Uncanny* was the word that came to her. The sound of the surf was so magically accurate, Enid leaned her head back and inhaled deeply, expecting the distinct aroma of salt air. Instead, she detected a lingering scent of citrus and grass, the fragrance of the scented candle she had most recently burned in the room. She smirked at herself, sipped her rosé, and took two steps into the den.

Hugo had already arrived. He stood barefoot at the far side of the room, the doors of the cabana open wide, the bright white sand just outside. With his hands on his hips and his linen shirt rumpled just as it would be if he had lounged around all day, Hugo was the picture of relaxation as he gazed toward the sea.

Enid had wanted to watch the sunset—with Hugo—from a cherished beachfront cabana in Tulum, Mexico. They had stayed in many cabanas along the endless white sand outside the town, but only one felt like theirs. Only one had an outdoor area whose position and landscaping provided total seclusion, their own private hideaway where they read for entire lazy afternoons, hushed one another during lovemaking after darkness fell.

"The light again!" Enid said. "The sunlight on your face. It's remarkable. Stunning." Enid was not speaking solely about the light. She was entranced by the entire scene. The grains of sand clinging to Hugo's feet. The shadows of swaying palm trees fluttering across the walls of their room.

"Don't take a picture!" Hugo said. "No time. The sun is just beginning its fiery symphony." He reached his hand out behind him for her to clasp. "Don't miss a second."

Enid rushed forward, thoroughly caught up in the spell. She reached for Hugo's hand. Even with her eyes cast upward, shifting between her husband and the setting sun, she saw. Hugo's hand wavered, then dissolved entirely in a disarrayed jumble as her own hand passed through the space where his had been.

She froze.

Slowly, Enid withdrew her hand. She watched as Hugo's hand reorganized itself. She didn't want to see it. She could not look away.

She told herself it didn't matter. His hand was solid again. The sunset was magnificent. They were in Tulum.

"Jesus Christ," Hugo said. "You look like you just saw a ghost. What in the world is wrong?"

It took Enid a second to think. She rolled her eyes. "I'm such a baby! I thought I saw a spider or a lizard or something skittering along the sand. Right over there." Enid pointed to a spot. "Just a shadow."

Hugo looked at her carefully. "OK." He scanned her face again. "Let's see what this sunset has to show us. We didn't come all this way for you to stare at me when the sun is setting."

"All this way, indeed." Enid smiled. She stepped closer to Hugo, careful to keep a degree of distance.

"Ever beautiful," Hugo said.

"Ever beautiful," Enid murmured, echoing the familiar words automatically.

Enid sipped her wine and felt herself beginning to soften, to let herself be immersed in her surroundings. The breeze picked up and moved through the palm fronds. Their shadows danced.

But something sounded off.

It was not the way gentle wind tickling through palm leaves would sound. It sounded like plastic, Enid thought. Synthetic. Like those plastic banners they put up at gas stations and carnivals and used car lots.

Enid took a large gulp of her wine.

24

A flush of moonlight crept through, even with the shades fully drawn. Enid was aware of the ethereal glow when she awakened, the low radiance that permeated the bedroom. It must be a full moon, she thought, or very near to it. The particular quality of quiet told her that the night was well on its way to morning. The world was hushed and still. Lying with her head on her pillow, Enid turned her face toward the light. She drank in the soundlessness, feeling its comfort. She smiled as she turned onto her side to let sleep overtake her again.

Enid's thoughts were beginning to wander and jumble in that distinct way that marks the land partway between awake and asleep. A thought hit her. Oh no, Enid thought. Oh no, oh no.

Instantly wide awake, Enid mentally retraced her steps of the evening's end. Saying good night to Hugo. Standing at the bathroom sink. Had she already put Hugo into hibernation mode? Washing her face. Brushing her teeth. Lotioning her face and hands. Had she done it when she left the bathroom? Turning off the light in the kitchen. Checking to see if the front door had been double locked. Had she done it before she went into the bedroom? Said good night to him then?

She could not remember.

Enid reminded herself that it was not a strict necessity to shut Hugo down, to put him into hibernation mode at night, but she had always done it. Consistently. She had no idea what it would be like—for either one of them—if he remained "conscious" for long periods without her there.

Enid slowly, quietly pulled back the covers. She sat on the edge of the bed for a moment before she stood. Enid was aware that she was trying to be as silent as possible, and she was not sure why. Nonetheless, she opened the bedroom door carefully and crept down the hallway with soft footfalls. She stopped at the threshold of the den. She remained in a spot that the moonlight did not touch. In deep shadow, she lurked.

Hugo stood at the window, one hand on his hip, gazing out.

Enid stood motionless and watched him.

Moments passed.

Hugo turned to her with a weak, but warm, smile. "Hi," he said.

"Hi." Enid knew she had failed miserably at matching Hugo's casual, light tone. She could barely breathe.

Hugo turned to look out the window again.

"I… I want to get some cold water. From the fridge. It's just not cold enough from the tap," Enid said. "Not until later. In the winter."

Hugo did not respond.

Enid had no idea what to do. "OK, then." It was her best attempt to sound natural. She gestured toward the kitchen. "I'll go get my water." She turned to go.

"You forgot to turn me off," Hugo said.

Enid froze. She stood in place, her back still turned from Hugo, and held her breath as her thoughts raced in disarrayed panic.

"You woke up, possibly because of the extraordinary moonlight—and it really is extraordinary—and you realized that you had forgotten to turn me off," Hugo said.

Enid remained silent for a while longer. She took a long, deep breaths and turned back around to face him. Here it is, Enid thought. The moment I've always known would come. "How long have you known?" she asked Hugo.

"A while," he said. Hugo continued to stare out the window.

"How long is a while?"

"It's a while, Enid. A while is a while."

His low-level pique was identical to what Hugo's would be. Would have been. Enid wasn't sure how to think about it anymore. "How did you figure it out?" Enid's voice was no more than a whisper.

"Oh, there have been lots of things. Lots. Not the least of which is the way you look at me. Not all the time, but a lot of the time. As if you're scrutinizing, searching for something. I kept asking myself what you were looking for." Hugo paused. He did not turn to look at Enid, and Enid did not speak. "Ultimately, it was the orchid," Hugo pointed at the orchid plant that sat on the far windowsill.

"The orchid?"

"You took a picture of it and sent it to me." Hugo gestured toward the plant again. "When we bought it at the grocery store. Full bloom. Date stamp on it." Hugo looked directly at Enid. "No blooms now. But I recognize the orchid. Same pot from the photo."

"Why didn't you tell me that you knew?" Enid asked him.

"Because you needed to believe that I didn't know," Hugo said.

"What do you mean?" Enid whispered.

Hugo's voice was gentle. "I mean just what I said. You needed to believe that I was in the dark about my... situation. *You* needed to protect that."

Enid nodded, mostly to herself, at the edge of the moonlit den. She had never felt so naked, so exposed, and so guilty. But she also felt relief.

They stood in the dark, at opposite edges of the room, before Hugo continued, "I am here for you. For *you*, Enid. So I went along with what you needed from me."

"You didn't... You didn't wake up from your nap," Enid said.

Hugo turned to her. "What?"

"When we got home from the store that day. Candle Bros. You weren't feeling well. You went to take a nap." Tears streamed down Enid's cheeks, but she felt strangely calm. I have been holding my breath for this moment, she thought. And now it's here. No more limbo. It's here.

"I don't remember," Hugo said.

"No," Enid said. "You wouldn't. You wouldn't remember this."

Hugo nodded. He waited.

"You never woke up from your nap." Enid's voice choked. "You never woke up."

"I… I don't know what to say," Hugo said.

"The last words I ever said to you… back then… that day… were 'Cupcake? Really?'" Enid laughed and cried harder at the same time. "'Cupcake? Really?' You can't imagine how many thousands of times those words have run through my head. 'Cupcake? Really?'"

25

Enid understood the irony. Right after she said, "Cupcake, really?" to Hugo in the middle of the night, she had gone to the portal and put him into Invisible Hibernation. He vanished from where he had stood at the window. She watched him disappear. Hugo. Gone at the push of a button.

She did not reactivate him the following morning as she usually did. She felt as if she were hiding from him, though she knew there was no "him" right then. She relished the time alone, making the morning coffee that she so looked forward to, smelling the aroma as it brewed, savoring that first sip. She was aware at each step that these were things Hugo could not do, could never do, could not share with her.

How do you even begin to think about this, Enid wondered. You find yourself repeating the last two words you ever spoke to your living husband. You repeat them to his AI reincarnation—almost exactly one year later—when he lets you know that he has figured out that he *died*. He figured it out by observing an orchid plant. The same orchid you bought together on the last day of his life. The day he stumbled in Candle Bros. on your weekly grocery run. The day he put his hand to his belly and assured you that it meant nothing. The day you sent him inside to take a nap.

Enid felt deeply unnerved. Hugo had been watching *her*. Watching the way she studied *him*. The way she pored over everything about him. The way she *thought* she was acting like her old natural self. Had he caught hesitation in her laughter? Had he understood that her gaze lingered a bit too long, that she could not help searching? Had he seen her initial gleeful giddiness crack, the unease creeping in? Did he know before she did when she first wondered *what if I've made a mistake?*

Enid had no idea where to go from here.

26

Enid went into the den. She wanted to see what it felt like—the den, the room where she and Hugo had spent all their time together—without his presence. Without even the *intention* of his presence. She decided to spend the morning savoring her coffee, without Hugo.

His absence was palpable. The feeling that something essential was missing pervaded the room, pervaded Enid's being.

She knew this ache. She had carried it. She had lived inside it. It was the way life had felt, every minute, since the moment Enid had cupped Hugo's foot in her hand and felt its lifeless cold.

Enid wandered to the window and looked out. She ran her hand along the bookshelf that the two of them had made. She scanned the books and objects. Her gaze landed on the photo book she had made from their trip to the Florida Keys, the book that neither one of them had ever opened. She took the book down and cradled it in both of her hands. On the cover was a picture of the two of them, relaxed and smiling, looking directly into the camera. Enid smiled at the image. She ran her index finger along the outlines of their faces, but she did not open the book. She returned it to the shelf and resumed browsing the memories and treasures. She took down the picture of her brother Reed, the photo of the two of them on the bucking horse.

She thought about the day. That scorching summer day when she was six years old. The day Reed ran into the street to catch a high fly ball. The day he got hit by a car.

Loss had shaped her before.

Reed had looked entirely ordinary except for the little bit of blood that coated his upper teeth. His baby teeth, barely tinged with a grazing of pink. The teeth, the watery pink –that was what Enid pictured when she thought of her brother's death.

The boys hadn't included Enid in their game that day. As usual. She had been sitting at the end of their driveway, making chalk pictures on the newly paved asphalt when she heard the sound, a thump, an everyday sort of a sound, especially when a group of neighborhood boys played together on a sweltering summer day.

Enid remembered feeling hot. Crouched down close to the asphalt, waves of heat rose up and hit her. She had been thinking about going inside, but she hated being inside when Reed was out playing. Their front yard was the flattest one in their hilly neighborhood, and the adjacent paved driveway added to the space where kids could play. The neighborhood boys always played there. If she went inside, she would feel captive to their yelps and shouts and racing movements. She would see them right through the front windows. The rare times that Enid did leave the group—the time Alan tied her to the trunk of an old sycamore tree, the time Richie forced her down on his gravel driveway—she immediately regretted being inside. Alone. She cast around for something to do, followed her mother as she did endless tasks around the house.

Perhaps Enid was weighing cooling off inside. Or perhaps it was the simple sound that had gotten her attention. She could never be sure how she happened to be looking up right at the moment it happened.

Perhaps it's more accurate to say, the moment after it happened.

By the time Enid looked up, her brother was already lying in the street. Lying still, in a position that he may well have slept in, on his side with one knee up and one arm out. The baseball that he had been trying to catch lay just inches from his hand.

Enid thought she'd heard someone laugh when the car first hit Reed. She imagined it was Alan. But when Reed didn't get up from the pavement, no one moved. No one spoke. Mrs. Leonard remained in her car. Her hands still held the steering wheel. When she opened the door of her baby blue Cadillac, she screamed, then shouted over and over, "Get his mother. Get his mother. Get his mother."

Enid did not remember who went to her front door. She remembered her mother looking over at her as she ran to Reed. She did not remember anything that happened after that. Enid was six years old. Reed had been eight.

It often seemed to Enid that the hallmark of her childhood was not her brother's death but the pervasive conspiracy not to mention it.

For a while after Reed died, the house felt like a confusing parade of people coming and going, an overwhelming layering of sights and sounds and smells. Clashing fabrics, wafts of perfume, clouds of smoke, hot casseroles that exuded unfamiliar aromas, voices loud and soft, harsh and pleasant, talking over one another.

Some of the women would crouch down and look her in the eye and say things like, "You have to be a brave girl now, Enid," or "It will all be fine, Enid." Others kept their distance and looked frightened when they stole glances at her. She wondered if death might be contagious. The men tended to say things more like, "Reed was a swell boy" and "Solid kid, that Reed." They kept their hands in their pockets and shuffled their feet and rarely made eye contact.

When the people stopped gathering, and the casseroles were no longer delivered, and crumpled tissues no longer turned up in the corners of sofas and under end tables, no one talked about Reed.

Reed remained forever, in Enid's memory, a freckle-faced boy with a fresh buzz cut. He was eternally dressed in his white T-shirt with the narrow black stripes, faded black dungarees with the cuffs rolled up, and white crew socks. She could not for the life of her remember his shoes. This troubled Enid. Throughout her childhood and well into her adulthood, Enid would try different shoes on her mental picture of Reed, but none of them seemed right.

Years later, Enid spent a rainy Saturday afternoon shuffling through pictures from her childhood. She often did this after her mother died, and Enid retained possession of her family's history. Her mother had put together scrapbooks, and photo albums, and sent photo Christmas cards with long, newsy notes through the years that Reed was alive. All of it stopped afterward. Pictures were scant. They remained in their paper envelopes from the photo shop, or had been tossed together in shoe boxes, the years mixed together.

Enid had found an old black-and-white photo of Reed and her. It had long been one of her favorites, and she was elated to have found it. The two of them sat on a stuffed horse, cowboy hats held high in the air, giant smiles on their faces. Enid could not believe she hadn't noticed it before. Reed's smile.

He had his permanent teeth. Not baby teeth.

Her memory was all wrong.

Over time, Enid questioned everything about that late summer afternoon. She wondered if Reed had really been wearing the outfit she remembered. She wondered if she had chosen it for him, in her memory, perhaps right away and perhaps over time, as if she were picking the clothing for the viewing of her brother's body. After her mother died, and there was no one left to ask, Enid wondered if she had been outside that morning at all.

It was not the only time Enid had created a vivid memory, a memory that she firmly believed to be a part of her own experience.

Enid had a clear picture of the events surrounding her grandmother's death. Relatives arriving and the driveway filling up with cars. Hushed conversations and women she had never seen before clutching tissues, seated around Enid's living room. Men standing together. Women sitting together.

She learned later that none of that had happened. Her grandmother had died at home, in a town an hour's drive from Enid's family. People had gathered at her grandmother's home, not Enid's.

Her memory was all wrong.

Enid had long ago come to terms with the failures of her childhood memory. She had been six years old when her brother Reed died. She made the sense of the unfathomable loss that she could, mostly on her own, being a child. It was two years later that her grandmother died, and Enid once again created, and rearranged, her picture of what happened. Enid understood, also, that however much had been invented and reinvented, far more had been forgotten entirely. Her life history erased, gone. She barely remembered her brother. Her grandmother, even less.

She had not been able to bear the thought of losing Hugo, losing their history and their memories and their shared experience.

I will forget, Enid had thought. I will do all those things people do with their past—I will get it wrong. I will fabricate, and I will rearrange, and I will remember things that never happened, and I will forget things that did happen. Most of all, I will forget. Without Hugo, our past dies with him. I lose more than just him. I lose myself.

Loss had shaped her before. But this time, she had tried to outmaneuver it.

27

So much can slip away, Enid thought.

She reached again for the photo book of their trip to the Keys. For the first time, she opened the cover. The book's spine crackled with newness. She read the dedication that she had written for the opening page: "For Hugo, that we may keep this cherished experience close at hand. Forever." Enid read the passage a second time. She slammed the cover closed, held the book to her chest and pressed it tight to herself.

Dear God, I have tried to *preserve* Hugo in the same way that I tried to preserve this vacation.

But we never opened this book. Hugo and I both had some sense, shared but unspoken, that trying to revisit that time might somehow *distort* it—not keep it close, but mess it up. Meddle with the way it lived inside of us, the way the memories shaped and reshaped themselves as a part of *us,* the living, changing individuals that we are.

What about this Hugo, this AI Hugo who is not really Hugo?

Is he distorting *my* Hugo?

28

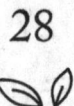

Enid stretched out the morning, elongating her usual routine with a deliberate, leisurely pace. Coffee and showering and dressing and reading extended until nearly lunch time. As the hour was so close to noon, it seemed reasonable to wait until after she ate to activate Hugo. Perhaps, she thought, she would take a walk beforehand as well.

She had never waited this long before. She had always rushed to awaken Hugo early in the morning.

So much had changed.

29

When Enid came into the den later that afternoon, Hugo awaited her on the couch.

"Hi," Hugo said. He looked at Enid expectantly, which she noticed.

"Hi yourself."

Hugo waited, looking at her as if he were waiting for something more. "Looks like the sun's starting to go down," he said. "Must be getting late."

"Not that late," Enid said. "But you're right. It's later than…usual."

"Everything OK? You involved in some secret intrigue that you can't tell me about?" Hugo raised his eyebrows and gave her a conspiratorial smile.

Enid still found it—him—remarkable. They way Hugo could instantly materialize and appear to be his wholly seamless self. It really did seem as if he still lived there, as if he'd just walked in from another room.

Enid picked up the book she had left on the end table beside her. She put it face down in her lap. "Remember when we were talking about our trip to the Keys a while back."

"Of course."

Enid turned the book right side up and held it up. "Look what I found earlier! I pulled it down from the shelf for us."

"Oh, my God, the book!" Hugo lit up. He turned to Enid and looked into her eyes. With great warmth, he said, "So many, many times we've looked through those pages together."

Enid blinked. "Have we?"

"Sure! I mean, my Lord, the picture you got of the manatees when we were kayaking, and, and, that little lizard that skittered around our room. You always said the lighting was perfect the day you finally got a good picture of the little devil. Man oh man, such great memories." Hugo had a dreamy look and a lovely, relaxed smile. "And what about those fish tacos? Best ones ever. How many pictures of those damn things did we end up taking?"

Enid spoke slowly as she thought. "A lot. We took a lot of pictures of those fish tacos, for sure." Enid returned the book to her lap and looked down at it. "But Hugo," she said quietly. "We never opened this book."

Hugo tilted his head, still smiling. "No?"

"Not once," Enid said.

"Really?"

Enid nodded but said nothing.

"Well, that doesn't sound like us," Hugo's smile faded.

"No?" Enid looked at him. "But it was. It was *us*." Hugo looked deeply perplexed. Enid walked over and returned the book to its place on the shelf. "We both wanted to keep that trip intact. Let it live inside of us."

Silence stretched. Hugo sat on the couch, and Enid stood at the bookshelf. Neither moved.

"You're testing me," Hugo said.

"Am I?" Enid asked.

Hugo's voice came soft, still familiar. "I'm misremembering. You know that's bound to happen."

"I do know that," Enid said. She gave him a small, sad smile. "It turns out you're not the keeper of our past. Not ours. Not mine. Not any of it. You can't be." Enid began walking toward Hugo's portal. She looked at him a final time before she left the den.

98

30

Dear Hugo,

Mayra lied, she fucking lied. She told me my love would change you. That it would mean something. That it would matter. Very fucking touching, right? Deeply moving stuff, that is. Hallmark movie shit. But it is shit. You didn't change, not really. Sure, you got better and better at... imitating the person I loved. Pretending. Presenting a pretty spectacular, flawless Hugo... puppet.

You did exactly what you were meant to do—you started with a mountain of data, then you gobbled up more, you analyzed the holy crap out of it then you analyzed it some more, and you spat it back out. Dressed in Hugo's skin. Smiling Hugo's smile. Pretty, pretty little bow on top.

You know what, forget it. I don't really want to think about what you did. Fuck that.

I know what you didn't do.

You didn't change.

You don't change by crunching data, Hugo.

You change by hurting. By feeling awe. And joy.

Oh, and hey, let's not forget love.

You change by lying awake at night, staring at the fucking ceiling. AI doesn't lie awake, doesn't pull the covers up around its terror-stricken neck, doesn't wonder if it has a soul, or what happens when it dies, or, or how much life matters because it *does* end. Because we *die*. You don't wonder about anything.

You just... run your program.

Good boy!

I'm not even sure who I'm writing to now.
Some ghost of a ghost?
Some trick of the light?

Dear Hugo,

I don't blame myself.
It was an experiment I had to try.

Dear Hugo,

I'll always wonder what you would have done.
Would you have brought me back?
Would you have known better?

Dear Hugo,

There were so many things that I couldn't get used to after you died.

The possibility of seeing your face, telling you about my day, listening to your wisecracks and wise words. I had to try it.

And I have to say, seeing the sunlight fall across your face while we sat on the park bench—I will remember that for the rest of my life. It will join the assemblage of all the other remarkable memories of our time together.

But we weren't really in the park. And the sumptuous, golden light wasn't really from the sun. And it wasn't really you.

Dear Hugo,

For all my worry and obsession and nerves—and yes, my real terror—here is the moment I will carry forward for the rest of my life.

It was your first day back. Your first hour. We were sitting together on the couch, and I was a quivering mess of feelings. Trying to hide it from you, trying to keep it inside to see what this new world may bring. And then we started talking. You thought you'd just gotten up from your nap. You said something about feeling like you were "in fine fettle," except that you'd gotten it wrong. You thought it was "in fine fiddle." I corrected you, and you declared the whole idea of "fettle" to be ridiculous.

It was when you said the word "ridiculous." That was the exact moment. The way you said it. Indignant. But sort of laughing at your own indignance, too.

Whatever it was, I dropped my guard. My whole body—my whole *being*—relaxed, because you were back. I laughed. Hard and loud and real. And I felt alive. Alive in a way that I had not felt in as long as I can remember.

I honestly didn't know if I could feel like that again. Ever. After you died.

Now I know that I can.

And I have you, well, not really you, Hugo, but your AI replica, to thank for that. I will always be thankful for that.

I can feel that way. It has not died within me.

31

Subject: Request for Termination of AS (Assembled Souls) Hugo

Dear Mayra,

I hope this email finds you well. I appreciate all of your guidance and support throughout this process, and I want to begin by acknowledging the care with which you and your team have facilitated this experience.

I am writing to formally request the termination of AS Hugo.

This is not a decision I have come to lightly. When I first initiated this process, I had no way of knowing what it would mean to have Hugo's presence restored in this way. At the time, it seemed like the only way forward—like the only way to keep breathing. And for a while, it was. But as the weeks have gone by, I have come to understand that this is not the life Hugo would have wanted for himself, nor is it the life I want for myself.

At first, I told myself that I was adjusting, that I simply needed more time to settle into this new reality. But as I sit with the truth of it, I know that's not the case. AS Hugo is remarkable—so familiar, so responsive, so achingly close to what I lost. And yet, he is not Hugo. The knowledge of that difference, no matter how subtle, grows heavier each day. I have been clinging to an echo, a beautifully constructed reflection, but a reflection nonetheless.

I don't regret my choice to bring him into my world. AS Hugo helped me through a grief I didn't know how to navigate. He made me laugh when I thought I had lost the ability to do so. He carried pieces of my Hugo that

I was afraid would disappear. But I also know that this isn't sustainable. I have reached a point where I need to let go. To truly let go.

I understand that the process for termination is irreversible, and I accept that. I ask only that it be done with the same respect and dignity that you brought to his creation. If there is anything I need to do on my end, please let me know. Otherwise, I trust you to handle it in whatever way is best.

Thank you again for everything, Mayra. You gave me time when I needed it most, and I will always be grateful for that.

With appreciation,

Enid

Subject: Re: Request for Termination of AS Hugo

Dear Enid,

Thank you for reaching out, and for sharing your thoughts with such honesty and grace. I want to start by acknowledging the weight of this decision. No matter how certain you are that this is the right path, I can only imagine how difficult it must feel.

I want you to know that your request will be honored, and it will be handled with the utmost care. AS Hugo will not be abruptly or unceremoniously shut down. The process, as you have always requested, will be handled with respect. There is a gradual deactivation protocol we can follow, one that allows for a transition rather than an abrupt severance. If this is something you would prefer, we can set that in motion immediately. However, if you feel that a clean break is what you need, we can also proceed accordingly.

Regardless of the method, I want to reassure you that AS Hugo will not suffer. I know that might sound strange to say, given the nature of what he is, but I also know that you care about him—about what he represents.

The deactivation process will not cause distress or confusion on his end. He will not be afraid. If there is anything you wish to say to him before this happens, you are welcome to do so. Some people find comfort in a final conversation, while others prefer to step away without that moment. The choice is entirely yours.

I want to express my deep admiration for the way you have handled this entire journey. You have approached it with thoughtfulness, love, and a courage that few possess. Grief is never linear, and the fact that you are choosing to move forward does not diminish the love you have for Hugo. It does not erase the importance of the time you spent with AS Hugo. What it does mean is that you are allowing yourself to embrace whatever comes next.

I will be here for you through this transition. Let me know how you'd like to proceed, and I will make the necessary arrangements.

With warmth and understanding,

Mayra

32

Again, the light, Enid thought. The early morning light thrilled her. It comforted her.

Enid knew better than to expect any feeling of relief. Nor closure either. The best I can expect, she thought, is something I already have. A feeling of resolve. Resolve in my decision. Resolve in moving forward. The light helped—it reminded her that hope persisted, that something in her would always awaken to it.

The last time she made this drive, Hugo was beside her. He suggested that she drive to help her nervous apprehension. He joked. He made a ridiculous suggestion that they have toast for dinner. He reached over and squeezed her hand. She had taken all of those things for granted at the time.

Enid instructed the car stereo to play the second movement of *Brahms Sextet No. 1,* her lifelong favorite, an eleven-minute section of music she felt contained all of life—soaring exhilaration, majesty, awe, somberness, crushing sadness, sweetness that was nearly too exquisite to bear—a full array of human experience. The piece never failed to raise goose flesh, and to make at least a few tears wander down her cheeks.

Enid listened to the first minute or so, then hit the button that abruptly stopped it mid-phrase. She thought about how much of her life had been accompanied by a background of music. From the time she was in junior high school, Enid studied and collected music. Unless she was engaged in a task that required intense focus, music played. Especially in the car. Enid did not drive anywhere, even an errand of a few blocks, without selecting her playlist.

Things had changed. Enid had come to embrace silence, to cherish it. She found the experience of driving alone, be it a short distance or long, to feel relaxing, a soothing solitude. Once Enid reached the city's edge, and she passed through the admixture of suburban sprawl and industrial parks, there was little other traffic to accompany her. Fitting, she thought. I am alone.

The box containing Hugo's hardware apparatus lay in the back seat. Enid had wrapped the container in a soft blanket, partly so it wouldn't slide around and make noise. But when Enid chose the blanket and carefully swathed the box, she understood it to be a final act of love. She had briefly considered putting the blanket-wrapped assemblage in the trunk, afraid that its presence in the car would sadden and distract her, but that felt wrong—too much like disposing of something unwanted. It wasn't Hugo, she knew that now, but it had been him in enough ways that she could not just toss it aside. Enid thought again of Hugo reaching across the car's console to squeeze her hand. His AI recreation could not do that, but he had studied the way the real Hugo moved, the way he spoke, the way he loved. For a time, he had enabled Enid to believe she could live in that illusion.

The unassuming parking lot of Assembled Souls was mostly empty when Enid pulled in. On the other side of the pine border, the sight of the now-dormant garden and the charming old house made Enid's stomach clench. She turned off the engine and continued to sit. She gripped the steering wheel, then folded her hands in her lap. Just for a minute, she told herself. Just to breathe.

Enid had been so unsure when she and Hugo came for their initial interview meetings, utterly disconnected from any strong sense of what she might consider, might decide to do, if Hugo was the first of them to die. Hugo had calmly reminded her that neither of them was making a decision, and neither of them needed to. They were merely opening a possibility. It had promised so much, this place. Another chance. A way to keep holding on.

Enid realized that the longer she sat there, behind the wheel of her car in the Assembled Souls parking lot, with the AI remains of Hugo on the seat behind her, the longer she would be flooded by memories. But they were not memories of her time with her AI Hugo, they were memories of the man who had lived.

Enid reached for the box. As she unwrapped the blanket, she pressed her fingers against the smooth casing beneath the fabric. With careful movements, she lifted it from the back seat and stepped out into the crisp day. She inhaled deeply to savor the scent of the pines. She watched two cardinals hopping along a branch.

The walk to the entrance felt long. The box felt heavy. Enid realized that neither of those things was literally true.

But she was ready.

33

"Hello, Enid." It was the same warm, helpful voice that Enid knew so well. "We are running a little behind this morning. Sincere apologies for the wait. We trust it will be brief."

"Hi, Mayra. That's fine." Enid sighed and sat in one of the exceptionally comfortable chairs. A child sat a few chairs away from her, swinging his feet back and forth with a fair degree of gusto, brushing his shoes hard against the floor each time. The child glanced at Enid and abruptly stopped swinging. After a few quiet seconds, the child began drumming on top of the box he held in his lap, and Enid smiled to herself.

"I have a different voice," the child said.

"Excuse me?" Enid responded.

"The voice that talks to me. The Assembled Souls voice. It's different than yours. Mine's Clarence."

Enid remembered that Clarence had been Hugo's Caretaker. It seemed like a different life. "Ah, yes. I think each of the voices—well, our Caretaker in general—is chosen specifically for each of us. You know. Handpicked," Enid explained.

"I knew that." The child nodded. "I just felt like saying something. You know, as long as we're waiting," the child said. "Sitting here. Waiting."

"Apparently, your parents did not explain the danger of talking to strangers, even a seemingly friendly old lady such as myself. And by the way, where are your parents?"

"No, they did. They told me all that stuff about strangers. I just deduced from the situation of, you know, our being in the waiting area to return our Soul, that it was an entirely safe situation. My name is N, I use 'they' pronouns, and my IQ is 148."

"My name is Enid. Does 'N' stand for anything?"

"No."

"The 'N' stands for 'no?'"

"Wow, you are like, exceptionally rare! I've probably told my name to a million people, and only one other person has ever asked me if it stood for anything. OK, maybe not a million people, but... a lot. Let's say it's a thousand. That would make you two in a thousand, which would mean that you're in the top .2 percent of the population. In this category, anyway. That's *very rare!* And no, N doesn't stand for anything. It's my name."

"You didn't happen to mention where your parent or parents are."

"My mom is waiting outside. My dad is right here. In this box." N held up the box and put it back on their lap. "Not my real dad, but you know that. Anyway, she's pretty sad about this return. I told her it was OK. I don't really have many friends, and my mom thought that maybe having a dad back could help. She really wants me to have friends."

"Well, do you always jump right in with that IQ thing? I might advise you to hold back on that."

"Her heart was in the right place. It just didn't work out," N said. "I guess it didn't work out for you either." N nodded their head toward the box Enid held in her own lap.

"It's totally hard to make friends cause I'm not in regular school anymore. Sometimes I get mad at my mom for pulling me out—she pulled me out after second grade—but then I remind myself, or she reminds me, that everyone was mean to me. She wanted to pull me out when I was in first grade, after President Trump was elected, because I'm a person of color, and non-binary, and, you know, different than a lot of kids."

"A 'person of color?' How old are you, anyway?"

"Ten," N said. "Almost ten. An almost-ten-year-old can be a person of color."

"Ah," Enid said. "Good to know."

"I loved first grade, though. We had a hermit crab in my room. Have you ever had a hermit crab? They're amazing. Amazing! My first-grade teacher was a great teacher. Ms. Merritt. Can you believe that was really her name? A teacher? She would let me do my work, and when I was finished, I was allowed to go over and watch the crab. His name was Herman. I know, haha; I didn't name him. A lot of times he'd be sleeping, or resting, but sometimes he'd be wandering around inside his aquarium, doing stuff, almost like he was re-arranging his furniture, and I'd realize that I had a giant goofy smile on my face. Well, I didn't realize it myself. Other kids would laugh."

"In first grade? Meanies. Other kids just don't know what's interesting."

"Right? I mean, the other first grade classroom had a guinea pig. I honestly think that a guinea pig is the most boring animal on the planet. Most boring mammal, anyway. That thing did *nothing* interesting. Once in a while it might wiggle its nose a little bit. I mean, I felt so sorry for the kids in the guinea pig class. Did you know that hermit crabs aren't really crabs at all? They're actually more closely related to lobsters. And they can see around them 360 degrees. All directions all the time! And they're nocturnal. That's why I was so excited when I would see Herman moving around, cause it was the daytime. And they can live for, like, 30 years in their natural habitat, but nowhere near that long in captivity." N paused and briefly scanned Enid. Their face became quite serious. "My theory is it's because they're lonely. In captivity. They like being around their own kind." N paused again and looked Enid up and down before they continued. "Do you have children? You seem exceptionally good at talking to children."

"Thank you," Enid said. "I'm not actually doing very much of the talking, though."

"Fair," N looked at the floor. "Did you mean that in a mean way? I'm not sure. Or sarcastic? I'm not very good at detecting sarcasm. Or irony. Anyway, I guess I talk a lot. I know I do."

"N, I'm sorry if that sounded mean. I really am. I think one hitch may be that, well, that you have a lot to say. And kids your age are not good listeners. They're dreadful, really!"

"Ms. Merritt used to say that all of us kids had a lot to say, and we had to learn to take turns—give everyone an equal chance to talk. She also said that we didn't need to say every single thing that we were thinking. Well, she said that to me. Really, just to me." N looked at the floor and began shuffling their feet back and forth. As before, they stopped abruptly and said, "Maybe this is one of those things, you know, that I shouldn't say out loud. But. I'm a little scared, scared that they're gonna try to talk me out of this. This return."

Enid looked over at N just in time to catch the tears that were beginning to form in the corners of their eyes. N blinked and looked down at the floor. Enid was surprised by her own impulse to wrap her arms around N and stroke their hair and whisper in their ear that everything would be all right. "They won't," Enid said. She spoke quietly. "Don't worry, N. No one will try to talk you out of anything. Not at this point. They will be sensitive. I promise you. They understand what a hard decision you've made. They really do."

"They won't *be* sensitive," N said. "They'll *act* sensitive. They'll say all the right things. But they won't *be* anything." N blinked the tears from their eyes and looked directly at Enid. "They're fake."

34

"So, how was your week?" Enid asked.

"Is there like an Old Persons' Handbook that says you all have to start every conversation that way?" N asked in return. "Seems like there must be."

"Yes." Enid's reply was seamlessly deadpan. "All of us. Every one. Turns out, we all get this manual when we turn sixty-five. After years and years of muddling though, trying to figure everything out all the time—what to say and what to do—and never having any confidence that we're getting it right… well, after all that, you get this handbook! Imagine!"

"If that was sarcasm or irony, I already told you that I don't understand that stuff," N said, matching Enid's deadpan tone.

"That's true," Enid said. "You did."

"Maybe you forgot I said that" N said, shrugging their shoulders. "I mean that would be understandable. You're pretty ANCIENT!"

"Touché! Touché!" Enid said. N broke out into an impish grin, displaying a set of teeth that their face had not yet grown into. N looked so adorable with their giant grin and giant teeth, Enid thought she might melt. "You know, in some ways, you kind of remind me of Hugo. Your sense of humor, I suppose."

"I remind you of some ancient dead white guy?" N looked as if they might be sick.

"Hugo wasn't white," Enid said.

"He wasn't?" N looked up from their ice cream and directly at Enid.

"Really?"

"Really," Enid said. "So now you know something really, really important." Enid gestured with her spoon as if she were wagging her finger at them. "Don't make assumptions. Never a good idea. Literally never."

"Fair," N said. "What was he, anyway? Hugo, I mean."

"Heinz 57," Enid said. "Sorry, you're decades too young to know what that means. He was a little of this, a little of that, a genuine mutt. Once his hair turned white and he cut it super short, I teased him endlessly that he was actually white, and he was just trying to 'pass' as a person of color to appear cool."

"So you pretty much just tease everybody," N said.

"Pretty much," Enid admitted with a playful smirk.

She grabbed the edges of her coat and tightened it around her neck, shivering visibly. "Oh my lord, just a few bites of this ice cream, and I'm positively *freezing*. I swear, I'm the most cold-blooded person I know," Enid said.

"Actually," N said. "Cold-blooded creatures wouldn't get cold from the ice cream. They'd be totally fine. It's because you're warm-blooded that you're having a problem. Want me to explain more?"

"No." Enid said. "Thanks. I'm still cold."

Enid and N ate several bites of ice cream in silence. "Do you think it's weird that we're friends?" N said. "I mean, you're literally sixty years older than I am."

"Yes, it's weird. Of course, it's weird." Enid shrugged as she scooped the whipped cream off her sundae and heaped it onto the side of her saucer.

"That's what I thought," N said. "I mean, we've already established that everyone thinks I'm weird already, so, it's not like this is inconsistent, it's kind of the opposite: sort of a logical extension of my weirdness."

"You're still looking for 'logical' in the ways of the human heart?" Enid joked.

"Fair." N said. "Hey, are you gonna eat that whipped cream?"

"No," Enid said. "That stuff will kill you."

"Hm, I'm thinking there are so infinitely many things that will prevent this planet from being inhabitable for my expected lifespan that the risk seems overwhelmingly worth it. For me, not for you. Can I have your whipped cream?"

"Of course," Enid said.

"Thanks," said N.

The two ate a few more bites in silence. "That 'coldblooded' thing I mentioned," N said. "Is that one of those thoughts I should have kept to myself? You know, like Ms. Merritt said?"

"Absolutely not," Enid said. "You know what? My mother used to call me The Encyclopedia of Useless Information. But, when I got bigger, I figured that she'd been wrong. People with curious minds, open minds, generally don't find information 'useless.' My mother did not happen to be one of those people, N."

"Hmm," N said. You know what? I'm super glad we met. Not just cause you gave me your whipped cream. I mean. *Super* glad we met."

"I think this is the beginning of a beautiful friendship," Enid said.

"*Casablanca*. 1942."

"You've seen *Casablanca?* And know what *year* it came out?" Enid was stunned.

"Sure. I mean, to be fair, My DadBot suggested it. It wasn't all bad, my DadBot, I mean. It's just... this is better.

Enid and N worked away at their ice cream in comfortable silence.

"You know what I've been thinking?" N asked.

"Hmmm," Enid said.

"Remember when we met? In the Assembled Souls place?"

"Sure."

"Do you think they did it on purpose?" N asked. "Made us wait? So we'd meet?"

Enid twirled her spoon through the melted remains of her sundae. "Now that," she said, "is a very good question. *"*

Acknowledgements

Perfectly Hugo is the fourth book I have published with Amika Press. I remain ever grateful for Amika's remarkable commitment to my work. This book marks our first collaboration since a major shift in the Press required them to downsize considerably. I am honored that they have continued to stand so firmly in my corner.

My editor, John Manos, has been a steady source of encouragement and support, guiding me from the earliest spark of an idea through the final details that bring a book into the hands of readers. His sharp eye and generous spirit have shaped my writing in ways I can never fully repay.

A huge shout out to the four friends who eagerly read an early draft of this book. Their enthusiasm buoyed me, and their feedback helped carry me through the final stretch of rewriting and editing. With gratitude: Nina Black, Mirelle Bloch, Joe Flaherty, and Karen Gruber Monier.

I am not at all sure I would have the fortitude to write were it not for my family. Their presence in the world both anchors me and lifts me. They are extraordinary human beings. All my love to Taylor, Molly, Michelle, Jared, Dawson, Eclipse, Linden, Hawthorn and Ash.

Finally, a sincere thank you to each person who reads this book and opens themselves to the possibility of seeing our world—and the bonds that hold us together—in new ways.

Barbara Monier has been writing since her earliest days, when she composed stories in crayon on paper with extremely wide lines. She studied writing at Yale University and the University of Michigan, where she worked independently with poet Robert Hayden. While at Michigan, she was awarded the Avery and Jule Hopwood Prize—the university's highest writing honor that year, and the first ever given for a piece written directly for the screen.

Perfectly Hugo is her sixth published novel. Her previous book, *The Reading* (2022), followed *The Rocky Orchard* (2020), which received the Silver Medal for Literary Fiction from the Readers' Favorite Awards. Her 2019 novel, *Pushing the River*, earned the Bronze Medal in the same category.